# STRATEGIC THREAT

## FINNEGAN FIRST RESPONDER SERIES

### LAURA SCOTT

READSCAPE PUBLISHING, LLC

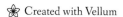 Created with Vellum

# CHAPTER ONE

Staff Sergeant Aiden Finnegan stood at ease dressed in his army dress blues. The cold November wind rattled the branches of the bare trees surrounding the Central Wisconsin Veterans Memorial Cemetery. He wasn't on duty today as a member of the Army National Guard. He'd come as a pallbearer and to pay his respects to his former commander, Sergeant Major Gregory Savage.

He surreptitiously watched the beautiful blonde Shelby Copeland née Savage wipe at her tears while holding the hand of a young girl roughly three years old. He'd met Shelby before as he'd served with her husband, Emmitt Copeland, before he'd been killed in the line of duty.

The young mother had lost her husband two years ago and was now attending her father's funeral. His heart ached for her. She looked fragile, pale, and alone standing in the cold as the pastor spoke of her father's dedication and service to his country.

Difficult to comprehend the man he'd long admired was dead. Sergeant Major Greg Savage had prided himself on staying in top physical condition. Even at the age of fifty-eight, the officer could keep up with the younger soldiers in his command. He and the other five soldiers chosen to carry the commander's casket struggled to understand how their sergeant major could have died of a sudden heart attack.

Yet here they were, burying the man with full military honors near his hometown of Oshkosh, Wisconsin.

When the pastor finished his brief sermon, Aiden allowed his gaze to roam over the oddly small group gathered at the grave site. He'd expected more attendees for a high-ranking sergeant major like Greg Savage. Yet some in the military deemed the National Guard to be less important than the regular branches of the armed forces—army, navy, air force, and marines. Oh, and the Coast Guard. The National Guard was not considered nearly as relevant. Until a disaster struck.

He watched as the bugler stepped forward, lifting the horn to his mouth to begin playing taps. The twenty-one-gun salute and folding of the flag would follow.

His eyes lingered for a moment on Shelby and her daughter. What was the little girl's name? Eva? The last time he'd seen the girl she'd been a baby. Shelby appeared stoic and somber, but the little girl looked around curiously, likely too young to appreciate the solemn event. Then he snapped to attention as the soldier with the bugle began to play.

The familiar notes hit him hard, as they always did. The scene was reminiscent of Shelby's husband's funeral, although there had been more attendees back then. He kept his gaze focused on the ground near Shelby's and Eva's feet. Once he'd imagined dedicating his life to the military, climbing the ranks the way Savage had.

But lately, he'd been considering a change. His current tour of duty was nearly over at the end of December. He'd originally planned to reenlist. Yet he hadn't signed the paperwork.

Maybe it was time to get out and search for a career with a regular schedule. The way most of his siblings were getting married, settling down, and having families made him keenly aware of his lack of social life. Frequent deployments made dating difficult. Maria had made it clear she was done waiting around for him. He couldn't blame her.

After the final notes from the bugle faded away, seven soldiers stepped forward, rifles resting on their shoulders for the twenty-one-gun salute. They would fire off three rounds. In choreographed unison, they lifted their weapons and fired into the sky.

Something kicked up a bit of the icy hard ground inches from where Shelby stood. Aiden reacted without thinking, lunging forward and grabbing Shelby and her daughter with his arms. He pulled them out of the way, using his own body for coverage.

The seven soldiers were already firing their second round before anyone seemed to realize what was going on.

"What are you doing?" Shelby asked in a choked voice.

"We need to get out of here! Now!" He ruthlessly pulled her up, then reached down to lift the crying toddler into his arms. "Hurry!"

The rest of the funeral attendees slowly began to rush forward. Thankfully, he had a head start. He pulled Shelby with him as he zigzagged through the tombstones to cross the frozen ground toward the line of trees.

"Have you lost your mind? What's wrong with you?" Shelby demanded.

"A bullet hit the ground near your feet." He continued moving through the foliage, sweeping his gaze around the area, searching for the gunman.

"It was probably from the twenty-one-gun salute!" Shelby yanked against his grip. "Let me go, Aiden. You're being ridiculous."

He wasn't, so he ignored her. Once they reached the shelter of the trees, he turned to look at her. "I saw the frozen ground kick up under the impact of a bullet. Someone took a shot at you under the cover of the salute honoring your father. The trajectory was such that it couldn't possibly have been from the seven soldiers firing into the air during the twenty-one-gun salute."

Her eyes widened, and she finally stopped tugging against him. Ignoring Eva's crying wasn't easy. He could hear the ruckus behind him and knew the other pallbearer soldiers back at the grave site were coming to find them.

He knew none of them could have fired the bullet he'd seen hit the ground, but that didn't mean one or more of them weren't involved.

As he'd anticipated, several of the funeral attendees caught up to them. He abruptly stopped, thrust Eva into Shelby's arms, and turned to face them. He lifted his hands to show he wasn't holding a weapon.

"Did any of you see the shooter?"

"What shooter?" Sergeant Oliver Kennedy asked. "What's wrong with you, Finnegan? Are you planning on holding Shelby and her daughter hostage?"

"No. I was getting them out of the way of the shooter." He outranked the soldier and did his best to level him with a stern glare. He didn't care that Oliver had been friends with Emmitt and likely knew Shelby better than he did. "Go back to the grave site. Inspect the ground where Shelby and Eva were standing. You'll see what I mean."

Kennedy exchanged glances with the others.

"I didn't see anything," Victor Morrison muttered.

"Fine, I'll go," Oliver agreed. "But Victor and the others are staying here to make sure you haven't lost your mind and are planning something stupid."

His jaw tightened at his subordinate's comment, but he didn't respond. Behind him, Shelby was comforting her daughter, and Eva's crying turned into sniffles. He lowered his voice and said, "Please stay behind me, Shelby."

She didn't respond, but she didn't move away either. He was glad she was taking his concern seriously.

A long, uncomfortable silence stretched between them. Aiden knew what he'd seen, and he wasn't about to back down despite the group of men and women facing him.

It seemed like hours instead of minutes before Sergeant Kennedy returned, his expression grim. "I found the area in the ground that you mentioned, Finnegan. I found the slug. It's not the same ammo used in the twenty-one-gun salute."

The discovery did not fill him with relief. Just the opposite. He didn't know who had come to the sergeant major's funeral to kill Shelby or why. "I need you and the rest of the team to spread out and search the area for the shooter. He's likely long gone but may have left evidence behind."

"Yes, sir," Kennedy replied, although the way he glanced at Shelby indicated Oliver would rather stay there to help protect the young mother. Victor, too, looked as if he didn't like leaving.

"Oh, and let the pastor and the other funeral attendees know the service is over," he added. "I'm taking Ms. Copeland and her daughter home."

Shelby sputtered in protest. He turned to look at her. "Do you want to put your daughter in danger?"

She pressed her lips together and shook her head. "Of course not. But there's no way that bullet was meant for me. Whoever fired it must have terrible aim."

"I disagree." To his mind, the bullet had come far too close. But her comment gave him pause. Soldiers were trained to hit what they were aiming at. So why had this shooter missed?

It didn't make sense. Especially because the assailant went so far as to use the twenty-one-gun salute to cover the sound of his own weapon. Then again, maybe the guy had been too focused on matching the timing of the rifles being fired into the sky rather than making the perfect shot.

"Let's get out of here." He put his arm around Shelby's waist, urging her across the hard ground toward the road where he'd left his truck. He doubted the shooter had stuck around, but he wasn't taking any chances.

"I have my car here." Shelby subtly pulled away from him. "I'll drive myself home."

"Not happening." He had to bite back a flash of anger. Striving for patience, he added, "Please, Shelby. I don't want anything to happen to you or Eva."

"You're taking this whole army obligation to Emmitt a little too far, aren't you?"

Aiden doubted she'd appreciate how his knowing her deceased husband had nothing to do with his motives. In truth, Oliver Kennedy and Victor Morrison were both closer to Emmitt than he was. "Emmitt would want me to look after you."

"Whatever." She suddenly sounded exhausted, as if the long funeral and the frantic rush from the burial had sapped her strength.

"I'll keep you and Eva safe." They reached the road where several of the funeral attendees were already in their respective cars, intent on getting out of there as soon as possible.

One soldier glared at him as he passed, as if the abrupt

ending to the solemn occasion was his fault. Aiden knew God had been watching over Shelby and her daughter today. He was just grateful he'd noticed the bullet striking the icy ground.

"We need to use my car." Shelby gave him a stubborn look when he paused near his cherry-red truck. "Eva's car seat is inside."

That hadn't occurred to him, although it should have. He'd taken Brady's son Caleb to the zoo twice over the summer and knew young kids needed to be in car seats.

"Fine. But I'm driving."

"I'm not in the military, Aiden, so stop ordering me around like I'm one of your soldiers," Shelby snapped.

He swallowed a retort and tried to soften his tone. "I'm sorry. The only reason I'd like to drive is to make sure we're not followed."

She sighed, then nodded. "You could have explained that up front. Clear communication goes a long way."

No argument there. Shelby led the way to a light-gray Jeep SUV, then opened the back to help Eva get inside. He stood behind her, scanning the area for any sign of a threat. When she finished, he opened the passenger door for her. "Keys?"

"I have the fob in my purse." Clearly, she had no intention of giving it to him. He closed the door behind her, then jogged around to slide in behind the wheel. Seconds later, he pulled out onto the road and followed the trailing cars out of the cemetery.

"Do you have any idea why someone would do this?" He glanced over to where Shelby sat, twisting her hands in her lap. She was dressed in funeral black, from her sweater and skirt to her heeled pumps and coat. "Why you've been targeted?"

"No!" Her raised voice was laced with fear. "It doesn't make any sense. I'm a teacher, not involved in the military like you and my father. I haven't done anything wrong. Why on earth would anyone shoot at me?"

It was a fair question. Too bad he had no answer.

———

SHELBY WANTED to cry but managed to maintain control for Eva's sake. At first, she'd wanted to believe this was nothing but Aiden Finnegan's overactive imagination. But then Oliver claimed to have found a mark in the dirt and a bullet. One that was a different caliber than the one the soldiers carrying out the twenty-one-gun salute were using.

And worse? It had struck the ground near the exact location where she and Eva had been standing!

"Maybe the, uh, attempt was meant for someone else." She turned in her seat, offering a reassuring smile for her daughter. Eva looked sleepy, no doubt tired from the long day too. The little girl probably didn't know what a bullet was, but she didn't like having this conversation in front of her three-year-old daughter.

"The pastor?" Aiden arched a brow. "Doubtful."

"Anything is possible." A theory she desperately wanted to believe. "Why not? Could be he has some dark, secret past. I sure don't."

Aiden frowned but didn't reply. She could tell he wasn't sold on the idea. But the more she thought about the near miss, the more logical it was that she and Eva were just innocent bystanders.

Not specifically targeted by a gunman.

Staring down at her hands, she imagined she could still

see the indentation from her wedding ring. She'd taken it off six months after Emmitt's death, but she hadn't dipped her toe back in the dating pool.

She wasn't interested in starting over. Besides, teaching and taking care of Eva took all her time and energy. Eva had just turned three, and her bundle of energy was both a blessing and exhausting. By the time Eva fell asleep, she was too tired to do anything else.

"Shelby?" Aiden's husky voice drew her gaze. "Are you okay?"

She shook her head but glanced pointedly back at Eva, indicating she didn't want to talk about it. He seemed to understand, and when he turned onto the highway, she noticed he'd headed toward Oshkosh. She inwardly sighed and relaxed, glad to know she'd be home soon. "I live off Sunset View Road, not far from the church."

"I remember." Aiden met her gaze. "I was there after Emmitt's funeral."

She glanced away. Sometimes it seemed as if Emmitt might walk in the door at any moment, coming home from a recent deployment. And other times she found it difficult to remember what it was like to be married. Their union had only lasted four years, and Eva had no memory of her father since he died just after her first birthday.

Aiden slowed and quickly moved into the right lane. She frowned, as this wasn't their exit. The way he kept his gaze on the rearview mirror made her stomach tighten. "Something wrong?"

"No."

The tense expression on his face belied his response. Twisting in her seat, she scanned the traffic behind her. He was driving at the speed limit, which most people didn't do. Car after car zoomed by, passing them on the left.

Was he doing this just to make her paranoid? Her gaze lingered on her sleeping daughter for a moment, then she sat back with a frown. Emmitt had told her Aiden was a decent guy to serve with. But other than meeting Aiden a handful of times—yes, including during Emmitt's funeral—she didn't know much about him.

Other than he came from a large family with something like eight brothers and sisters. As an only child, she couldn't imagine growing up with that many siblings.

She lurched in her seat when Aiden made an abrupt turn, exiting the interstate at the last possible second. Grabbing the handrest with one hand, she braced herself on the dashboard with the other.

Before she could ask what he was doing, he hit the gas, flying through a yellow light that turned red the moment they reached the center of the intersection. Car horns blared and a wave of anger hit hard. Eva was in the car! If they'd been hit, her daughter would be injured, or worse!

"What's wrong with you?" It was all she could do not to scream at him, but she did use her best stern teacher's voice, lowered so as not to wake Eva. "Pull over right now! I do not feel safe with you speeding like a maniac through yellow lights."

Aiden ignored her, weaving between cars before turning sharply and taking the on-ramp to get back onto the interstate. Only they were going the wrong way.

She smacked him on the arm, her knuckles brushing against the stripes on his uniform sleeve. A quick glance back confirmed Eva was still asleep. "Why are you acting like this?"

"There was a black SUV following us." His tense tone sent shivers down her spine. She twisted again in her seat but didn't see anything.

"Are you sure?"

"Yes." He shot her a concerned look. "It stayed in the middle lane but dropped his speed dramatically when I did. No one does that, Shelby. I had no choice but to bail."

She wasn't sure what to think. Her husband knew Aiden, along with several of the other men who'd been at the funeral today, so logically she should be able to trust him. But this—this couldn't be happening. There was no reason for anyone to follow or shoot at her!

Unless . . .

Pressing a hand to her racing heart, she forced the question past her tight throat. "Is this related to my father?"

"That possibility has occurred to me." Aiden didn't meet her gaze, his attention riveted on the rearview mirror. "I don't understand what's going on here, but I don't think you should go home. Not yet."

She glared at him. "I have to go home. I have school next week." Today was Thursday, and she'd been given Friday off as a bereavement day. But her principal expected her to be in her classroom teaching fourth graders on Monday.

His jaw tightened. "I don't care. It's too risky."

She was getting mighty tired of his telling her what she could and couldn't do. Pulling herself together, she lifted her chin. "Isn't it possible that you're overreacting? Just because some guy slowed down on the interstate when you did doesn't mean he was following us. Maybe he assumed you saw a cop?" She crossed her arms over her chest. "Take us home. Now. Eva will need a snack soon."

As if on cue, her daughter spoke up. "Mommy? I'm hungry."

"We'll be home soon, sweetie." She glared at Aiden. "Right?"

He shook his head as if frustrated, but then he exited

the freeway. This time, he didn't get back on the interstate but stayed on a rural highway. She wanted to snap at him again but managed to hold her tongue.

Now that she was thinking more clearly, the idea of her father somehow causing danger to show up here at his funeral of all places didn't make sense either. He'd dedicated his life to serving the Army National Guard. He was approaching his thirty years of service and had been scheduled for another promotion.

Besides, the role of the National Guard was to protect the public and provide assistance during natural disasters. It was the one branch of the service where soldiers were responsible for protecting the United States, rather than being sent abroad. That was hardly the sort of career that encouraged or supported criminal activity.

Aiden's stern features and long silence indicated he was angry. Too bad. So was she. This wasn't how she'd imagined her father's funeral would go.

"Mommy, I'm hungry!" Eva's insistent tone had her rummaging in her small purse for a bag of fish crackers.

"Here." She turned and gave the small baggie to her daughter. There would be orange cheese smears over everything back there, including Eva's face and hands, but she didn't care. "We'll be home soon. Right, Staff Sergeant Finnegan?"

He scowled. "Aiden. And yes, we'll be there soon."

Rubbing her temple, she let out a silent sigh. "I'm sorry," she murmured. "It's been a long day."

He shot her a surprised glance, then nodded. "I understand."

Seeing the church steeple up ahead, she estimated they were less than five minutes from her home. Her feet ached from her low-heeled pumps, more so after the mad dash across the cemetery to hide in the trees. She couldn't wait to get out of her funeral attire.

The thought of never seeing her father again hit hard. Not that he'd been around much when she was a kid, but later, after her mother had died, he'd done his best to balance his homelife with his career.

And after Emmitt had died, her dad had been her rock, helping as much as he could with Eva between homeland deployments.

"You have off tomorrow?" Aiden's question caught her off guard.

"Yes. I was given five bereavement days to plan and attend his funeral." She shrugged. "It would be nice to be off longer, but the Thanksgiving break will be here before you know it. I didn't want to use any more personal days." Another pang hit hard at knowing her father wouldn't be there for his favorite holiday of Thanksgiving.

Or at the upcoming Christmas holiday either.

Aiden passed her street. "You missed the turn."

"I'm going around the block as an extra precaution," he told her. "Eva's okay with her crackers, right? A slight detour isn't going to hurt anything."

"I guess not." She wondered again if he was doing this on purpose just to scare her.

After circling the block, he headed down her street. As Aiden drove toward her house, a small brown ranch building with large trees on either side, she wondered how he planned to get home as he'd left his bright-red truck at the cemetery.

That was his problem, not hers.

As her vehicle slowed, she caught a glimpse of movement along the side of her house. A shadow beneath her tree. Dusk was falling, so she wasn't absolutely sure she hadn't imagined it.

Until she heard the crack of gunfire.

Aiden hit the gas, the Jeep lurching forward. Eva started crying as she grabbed the handrest again as they took a sharp turn.

Then Aiden punched the accelerator, speeding away from her normally quiet and serene neighborhood.

Stunned, she couldn't believe what had just happened.

Aiden had been right all along. Someone really had tried to kill her!

# CHAPTER TWO

He'd known going back to Shelby's place was a bad idea. But he had not anticipated the gunman would be waiting for them. He'd hoped to have enough time to convince Shelby to pack a bag for herself and Eva so they could get out of there.

"I don't understand," Shelby whispered as he drove as fast as possible away from her house. "What's going on?"

"I don't know." He took several turns, dividing his attention between the road ahead and watching their six in the rearview mirror. He was glad they were in a gray Jeep, though. His cherry-red truck would have been far too noticeable.

"Mommy?" Eva's voice was laced with fear. Glancing at her in the rearview mirror, he saw she'd clapped her hands over her ears, orange cracker crumbs staining the blond tresses she'd inherited from her mother.

"It's okay, we're fine." He injected confidence into his tone, even though he had no idea where the threat was coming from.

"Mr. Aiden is going to take us on a little ride," Shelby

added, turning in her seat to smile reassuringly at her daughter. "Won't that be fun?"

Eva shook her head. "I wanna go home."

He hated knowing this innocent child was in danger. Shelby too. Once he hit the interstate, he headed south.

"Where are we going?" Shelby asked in a hushed tone.

"The American Lodge. It's a motel that isn't too far from the Finnegan homestead." At her confused look, he clarified. "My family home in Brookland."

Shelby tossed a worried glance back at her daughter. "Is it necessary to go that far? Brookland is an hour away from our home."

"Yes." He tried to soften his tone so she couldn't accuse him of barking orders. "I'm truly concerned about your safety, Shelby. My oldest brother Rhy is captain of the tactical team. His wife is pregnant, due sometime this month, so I can't risk bringing danger to their doorstep. But the motel is close enough that Rhy can drive over to talk to us. We need to decide our next steps in figuring out who is behind these shootings."

She frowned. "Shouldn't we call the Oshkosh police? Isn't it their job to investigate crimes?"

It was a good point. "You're right. It's important for them to be included. Call and report gunfire at your address. Let them know you and Eva are safe, but that you're too afraid to return home."

"Okay." She quickly made the call. He listened while she described the incident, adding there had been gunfire at the cemetery too. After listening for a moment, she said, "I understand. We'll be there soon to make a statement."

He shook his head as she disconnected from the call. "That's not happening. We can't stick around. I'm concerned the gunman will anticipate you showing up at the local precinct."

She bit her lower lip. "You make it sound like this guy has superpowers or something."

Or something. "Not superpowers, but he is determined to eliminate you as a threat." He glanced at her again. "You're sure you don't know why?"

She threw up her hands in frustration. "How could I? I'm a fourth-grade schoolteacher. That's hardly a career that invites violence."

"Any parents giving you trouble lately?"

She scoffed. "Seriously? You think a parent upset with their son's or daughter's grades is going to shoot at me?"

He had to admit it was far-fetched. Then again, she had been targeted by gunfire. Twice. He knew better than most how some people could be irrational and emotionally unstable.

Continuing south on the interstate, he took the next exit. After going a mile or so, he got back on the interstate, keeping an eye on the road behind him to be sure they weren't followed. Looking back, the black SUV that had braked when he had must have been following them earlier. When he'd gotten off the interstate, they likely continued on, knowing where Shelby lived and reaching the house ahead of them.

When he was finally certain they'd escaped without being tailed, he dug his cell phone from his pocket. His phone wasn't linked to the Jeep's computer, so he couldn't use the hands-free functionality. Using his thumb, he scrolled to Rhy's name and called his brother, placing the call on speaker.

"What's up, Aiden?" his brother asked.

"I need a favor."

"Of course." As the oldest of nine siblings, his brother Rhy had moved home along with his second oldest brother, Tarin, to hold the family together after they'd lost their parents in a tragic accident eleven years ago. Aiden and his twin Alanna had been seventeen at the time, and their youngest sister, Elly, only fourteen. The entire Finnegan family dedicated themselves to being first responders. "What do you need?"

"I'm with a friend, Shelby, and her three-year-old daughter, Eva. They're in danger. I'm taking them to the American Lodge, but I'd like you to meet with us to determine next steps."

"What kind of danger?" Rhy asked with concern. "What's going on?"

"Two episodes of gunfire. One at her father's funeral, the other at her home. We may need help with clothes and other items for them too."

"Maybe you should bring them to the homestead," Rhy said.

"Nope." He frowned. "It's not an option to put Devon and your baby in danger."

"Yeah, I hear you." Rhy sounded frustrated. "Okay, I'll call and get the rooms at the American Lodge squared away. We'll take care of clothes and other items once you get settled."

"Thanks, Rhy. We'll be there in an hour."

"Got it. Drive safe." Rhy ended the call.

"I hav'ta go to the bathroom," Eva announced.

He glanced at her in the rearview mirror. She was squirming in her car seat, indicating he needed to get off the interstate as quickly as possible. "Okay. Hang on. We'll get to the bathroom soon."

Thankfully, there was an exit with both a gas station

and truck stop diner. He left the freeway, then drove straight to the gas station.

"I gotta go right now!" Panic underlined Eva's tone.

He'd barely stopped the SUV when Shelby jumped out and opened Eva's door. She had the little girl out of the car seat in a flash, hurrying her toward the building. He needed to put gas in the tank but threw the gearshift into park and killed the engine. He slid out of the Jeep and followed them inside, just to be safe.

Standing near the restroom doorway, he could hear Shelby taking care of her daughter. "You can't always wait until the last minute, sweetie. You need to tell me you have to go ahead of time."

"I did," Eva insisted. Aiden found himself smiling at her logic. A minute or two probably seemed like a long time to a three-year-old.

"Okay, let's wash up. You're orange from head to toe."

Several customers walked by, eyeing him curiously as he stood in his dress blues outside the restroom. He made a mental note to have Rhy bring him a change of clothes too. Wearing his formal uniform brought undue attention.

Something he'd rather avoid.

When the bathroom door opened, Shelby looked surprised to see him standing there. He took a step back, then gestured at the store shelves. "Is there anything you'd like to buy?"

She frowned, then shook her head. "Nothing here. My feet are killing me, though."

"My family will help get us a change of clothes, shoes, and whatever else you need." He took a step forward. "Two things. I need you to ditch your phone. And to stay behind me at all times. Okay?"

"My phone?"

"It could be tracked." He gave her a sympathetic look. "Please."

She huffed but went ahead and powered down her phone, then dropped it into the trash. When they passed a small toy section, Eva grabbed a doll. "I want this one."

"You have dolls at home," Shelby reminded her.

"But we can't go back there yet," he said in a low voice. "If you don't mind, I'd like to buy it for her."

Her scowl indicated she wasn't thrilled, but she nodded. "Only this once, though. She can't have everything she wants."

"Understood." He'd experienced that with Brady's son, Caleb. The kid wanted everything in sight, and when he had to choose only one thing between everything the gift shop had to offer, it had taken the six-year-old an unbearably long time to decide on the stuffed penguin. Chosen, no doubt, because of the way the siblings teased Kyleigh's husband, Bax, calling him Penguin.

He took the doll from Eva and carried it to the counter. He paid in cash, then ushered them out to the Jeep. He took another few minutes to fill the gas tank, then drove back onto the freeway.

In the back seat, Eva talked to her doll. To his surprise, Shelby reached out to rest her hand on his arm. "Thank you. For keeping us safe."

"Anytime." He swallowed hard, trying not to read more into her gratitude than he should. Shelby was beautiful, but as his subordinate's widow, she was way off-limits. And he also knew she wouldn't be interested in him that way.

Until now, they'd only been acquaintances. After all of this, he hoped she'd at least view him as a friend.

The rest of the trip to Brookland was uneventful. He had not noticed anyone following them, but he had taken a long circular route to the American Lodge motel just in case.

Shelby eyed the two-story white motel curiously but didn't protest. She lifted Eva out of the car seat and held her hand. "Stay with me."

"Okay." Eva held her new doll close as he gestured for mother and daughter to go into the lobby first. He recognized the former firefighter Gary Campbell behind the counter.

"Rhy told me to expect you," Gary said by way of greeting. "I have two connecting rooms on the ground floor." He pulled out two key cards and slid them across the counter.

"Thanks, Gary," Aiden took the keys, handing one to Shelby. "This is Shelby and her daughter, Eva. Shelby, this is Gary Campbell. He's a former firefighter turned motel owner."

"It's nice to meet you." Shelby's smile appeared strained. No doubt the events of the day were catching up to her. "Thanks for the rooms."

"Anytime." Gary waved a hand. "Finnegans and Callahans get a special discount."

"Callahans?" Shelby echoed in confusion.

"Our cousins." Aiden waved a hand. "Not important right now. Thanks again, Gary."

"Anytime," Gary repeated as they turned to leave.

Their rooms were located toward the end of the lower level. Gary had installed security cameras, and Aiden was grateful for the added layer of safety they'd provide. Not as good as the security system Rhy had installed at the homestead, but better than nothing.

"I think it's weird that your family gets special rates for a motel," Shelby said as he unlocked the door to her room. "Especially since you live in the area."

This probably wasn't the time to explain how much danger his family had faced over the past year. Not that their jobs as first responders didn't often put them in the line of fire, but his siblings had faced more than their fair share of danger.

Ironically, it appeared to be his turn to protect someone from danger.

Shelby kicked off her shoes with a soft groan. "I'm never wearing heels again."

He nodded in sympathy and tugged at his starched collar. "I get it. I can't wait to get out of this uniform."

She sighed and plopped down onto the bed. "I feel like I've stepped into a nightmare."

"I understand." He rested his hand on her shoulder, then glanced over to where Eva was dancing around with her doll. "Give me a few minutes to talk to Rhy, okay? He'll bring us food and a change of clothes."

"He has a three-year-old daughter too?" she asked.

"No. You'll need to make a list of what you'd like with sizes for both you and Eva." He crossed over to unlock the connecting door. "I'll give you privacy, but you also need to keep this unlocked in case I need to reach you in a hurry."

She paled but nodded. "Okay."

He dropped to his knees beside her. "Hey, try not to worry. I'm sorry you're going through this, but please know my only goal is to keep you and Eva safe."

"Safe from what?" Her wide blue eyes clung to his. "I don't understand what's going on. Nothing makes sense."

"I don't either. But several of my brothers are cops, and Brady is with the FBI. We'll figure out who's behind this."

"Eight siblings, right?" She shook her head. "Emmitt mentioned you had eight siblings."

"Including a twin sister." He offered a crooked smile.

"The good news is that family is important to us. We'll all work together to keep you and Eva safe."

"Okay, thank you." She appeared to pull herself together. "I appreciate everything you've done."

He patted her knee, then rose to his feet. "Make that list. Things will be better once we've eaten and are comfortable."

She nodded. As he waited, he found himself running through the events in his mind. A shooter had staked out her father's funeral and then shown up at her house.

He found it difficult to imagine a grade-school teacher making enemies, which had him thinking of her father.

And her deceased husband.

Back when Emmitt had died, there had been some rumblings about the shooting not being an accident. But the army investigator assigned to the case had not agreed. Now that Shelby had been targeted, he couldn't help wondering if this was related to Emmitt's death. Or something involving her father.

As far as her dad was concerned, it wasn't unheard of to make enemies in the armed forces. Even in the National Guard. Yet investigating a sergeant major and a former sergeant would not be easy. He didn't have access to military personnel records.

Would Brady? He wasn't sure the FBI could get what they'd need. He blew out a breath. One of these men had created an enemy who felt the need to eliminate Shelby and her daughter.

They just needed to figure out who and why.

A seemingly impossible task.

AS MUCH AS Shelby didn't like the idea of Aiden's family buying her clothing, the thought of wearing the uncomfortable dress shoes for any length of time was enough to have her making the list of things for them to buy. Thankfully, Eva was easy.

"Here." She thrust the scrap of paper at Aiden. "Tell your brother thanks from me. I'll pay him back once I'm able to return home."

"Don't worry about that." He took the list, then turned away. "Rhy? We're at the American Lodge. I'm texting you a list of things we need."

Shelby turned on the television, grateful to find a station with cartoons. Normally, she limited her daughter's screen time, but today was an exception to the rule.

Her thoughts returned to her father's funeral. Leaving so abruptly seemed wrong. Like she wasn't honoring him in the way he deserved.

Then again, if her dad was still alive, would this even be happening? She honestly didn't think so.

Turning from the cartoon, she caught Aiden's intense brown gaze on her. Her cheeks flushed with embarrassment. Why? She had no idea. It wasn't like her to be so keenly aware of a man.

"Do you and Eva like Italian?" he asked, the phone still to his ear.

"Yes, but make it something simple like spaghetti or pizza. She can be picky sometimes."

"No problem." Aiden's smile softened his features. "Spaghetti is perfect, thanks."

A minute later, he disconnected from the call. "Stay here for a few minutes. I need to get into my room and unlock the other side of the connecting door."

"Sure." She was touched that he'd cared enough to get

them two rooms. Emmitt had considered Aiden to be an honorable guy, someone he liked reporting to. After everything that had transpired today, she had to agree.

"I'm hungry," Eva announced again. "Dolly is hungry too."

"We're having spaghetti for dinner." She sat beside Eva along the end of the bed closest to the television. "One of your favorites."

"Yum!" Eva smiled as she held up the plastic doll. "Dolly likes spaghetti too."

She smiled, brushing a strand of Eva's light-blond hair away from her cheek. Now that the danger was over, her fingers trembled at the near miss. She'd never survive losing her daughter.

*Never.*

Hugging Eva close, she found herself whispering a silent prayer for the little girl's safety. Prayers hadn't come easy over the two years since losing Emmitt. She'd stopped attending church and had claimed she was too busy with her job and raising a small child when some of the parishioners had called to express their concerns over her absence.

She'd tried to attend services after Emmitt's death. But each time she'd taken her seat in the pew, her eyes would fill with tears. It wasn't as if Emmitt had always been able to accompany her to church on a regular basis, especially not while he was deployed.

But she'd stopped going just the same.

Glancing down at Eva now, she felt ashamed of how she'd pushed aside her faith.

"Everything okay?" Aiden's voice startled her from her thoughts. Eva squirmed out of her arms.

How could they be? She was sitting in a motel over an hour from her home because she'd been shot at twice.

As if reading her mind, Aiden came over to sit beside her. "Silly question, I know. But Rhy, Tarin, and Brady are all coming to meet with us. We'll talk things through and come up with a plan of action."

"Sounds good." She forced a smile. "I hope there's not a quiz. You've mentioned Rhy twice, but who exactly are Tarin and Brady?"

"I'll give you the rundown on the sibs. Rhy is the oldest, he's married to Devon who is pregnant with their first child. Tarin is a detective with MPD and is married to Joy, who is also pregnant. Brady is an FBI agent, and he's married to Grace. They have a six-year-old son named Caleb." He paused, then added, "Kyleigh is a Milwaukee County Sheriff's Deputy, married to ADA Bax Scala. Quinn is with the Coast Guard and married to Sami who is also a cop. Colin is a firefighter and is married to Faye, a doctor in the emergency department at Trinity Medical Center. My twin sister, Alanna, is a nurse at the same hospital; she's engaged to Reed Carmichael who is also a cop. And finally there's Elly, the youngest, who is an EMT."

"Wow. Lots of cops," she murmured.

"Exactly. Which is why I know we'll get to the bottom of this." He gave her a quick hug, then stood. "We'll eat first."

Despite the fear and worry, her stomach felt hollow with hunger. Probably because she hadn't eaten much prior to the funeral.

Aiden's phone buzzed. After reading the text message, he crossed over to peer through the window. "They're here."

The three Finnegan men shared similar facial features to Aiden. Tarin in particular shared the same red hair. She personally thought Aiden was the most handsome of the group, but maybe that was only because he wore his dress uniform.

Stupid to be swayed by a military uniform. After losing Emmitt, she'd vowed to stay far away from those who served in the armed forces. Easy enough to do since she wasn't ready to date anyway. And being a schoolteacher wasn't conducive to meeting soldiers.

After Aiden had introduced them, they all crowded into Aiden's room. He handed her the bag containing their new clothing, so she hurried to the bathroom to change. Aiden did the same, and she sighed in relief to have soft running shoes on her feet and comfy jeans to wear.

She, Eva, and Aiden sat around the small table while the rest of the Finnegans sat along the edge of the bed.

Aiden surprised her by bowing his head to say grace. "Dear Lord, we thank You for this food we are about to eat and for the way You have kept us safe in Your loving care. We ask for Your continued guidance as we take Your chosen path. Amen."

"Amen," she whispered.

Aiden's smile warmed her heart. As they ate, the three Finnegans spoke in low tones. Finally, Brady said, "I tried to dig into the sergeant major's background. Even as a federal agent, I'm not allowed to have access to his personnel records. I mean, I could request them if there was a reason to suspect suspicious behavior."

She pierced him with a sharp look. "My father wasn't involved in anything illegal."

Brady lifted his hands. "I never said he was. I'm just trying to understand why someone would target you at his funeral and again at your home."

Her shoulders slumped. "I don't know. But maybe you should look at soldiers who left my father's command under protest. Anyone who may have been dishonorably discharged."

"That's an idea," Aiden admitted.

"It is, but I don't know that I'll have access to that intel either," Brady said.

"I know a guy who transferred from the National Guard to work for army intelligence," Aiden said thoughtfully. "His name is Tom Mitchell. Maybe he can help us."

"Call him," Brady advised.

"We brought you new cell phones and cash too," Tarin said. He hadn't said much, making Shelby think he was the quietest one of the bunch. "You'll want to take precautions from this point forward."

Aiden nodded. "We used Shelby's phone in the car, then ditched it at a gas station. We should be safe here."

"I also brought a spare weapon from the gun safe." Her eyes widened when Rhy handed Aiden a gun and holster.

"You need to keep that away from Eva," she said sharply.

"Of course." Aiden took a moment to strap on the belt holster. "Okay, now that we have the basics covered, what else can we do to find this guy?"

"I'm digging into crimes that involve army service men and women," Tarin said. "Brady is doing the same but on a federal level."

"I'll chip in, too, but Devon is still on bedrest." Rhy looked apologetic. "She has a doctor's appointment tomorrow, and I have a feeling they're going to induce her."

"Since she only has three weeks to go, I think that's wise," Aiden said. "Don't worry, we can always call Kyleigh, Sami, or Reed for backup if needed."

The way Aiden's family jumped in to help made Shelby

realize maybe there were perks to having so many siblings. She figured Aiden was never lonely.

About an hour later, the Finnegans left. The small motel room was quiet without the three additional men sitting there.

"I should give Eva a bath." She helped Aiden clear away the mess from their spaghetti dinner. She smiled and added, "Pretty sure she still has fish cracker crumbs in her hair."

"That's fine." Aiden handed her the canvas bag of clothing. "They added some things for Eva. Toys and a change of clothes."

"Okay, thanks." She gratefully took the items. "We'll say good night, then. After Eva's bath, I'll put her to bed."

Aiden nodded. "Good night."

Oddly, she didn't want to leave him. Eva loved taking baths, though, so soon she had the little girl clean and dressed in footie pajamas. Perfect for a November night.

Shelby stretched out on the bed beside her daughter. Her mind whirled, but eventually pure exhaustion sucked her in.

It seemed like just a second later when she felt a hand on her shoulder and heard a male voice whispering in her ear, "Wake up. We need to get out of here right now."

What? She blinked at him through the darkness. His grim expression indicated this was no joke. She wanted to ask more, but he put a finger to his lips, indicating the need for silence.

She shoved her feet into the running shoes, then grabbed her coat. Aiden thrust the bag of clothing into her hands, then gestured to Eva. His gaze asked if she could carry the girl.

With a nod, she looped the strap of the canvas bag over

her shoulder, then carefully picked up the sleeping toddler. Eva protested, then snuggled against her.

Aiden drew her close, then edged to the door leading outside as a crack of gunfire shattered the silence of the night.

# CHAPTER THREE

Aiden felt certain his brother Brady had been the source of the gunfire, but he stayed inside the motel, weapon in hand. Thank goodness Gary had installed those cameras. The former firefighter had called Aiden to let him know someone was lurking in the woods, using night-vision binoculars to watch their motel room door. And the perp had been armed. Hearing this, he'd contacted Brady, knowing his brother was keeping watch nearby.

Clearly, Brady had found and flushed the shooter from his position.

After what seemed like an incredibly long minute, he heard a shout. "Aiden, you're clear!"

He let out a soundless sigh and reached for the motel room door.

"Wait!" Shelby gripped his arm. "Are you sure it's safe?"

"Brady has secured the area." He tried to smile reassuringly. "Stay close."

The darkness made it difficult to gauge the expression in her eyes as she gave a jerky nod. He opened the door, poked his head out, then crossed the threshold. Shelby followed, murmuring words of comfort to Eva.

Or maybe she was talking to herself.

He caught sight of Brady standing near Shelby's Jeep. His FBI brother's expression was serious. "I didn't hit the perp. Unfortunately, he took off. I didn't want to leave you and Shelby alone, so I let him go."

He squashed a flash of disappointment at hearing the perp had gotten away. Although he appreciated the backup. "Thanks for sticking around."

"I'm glad I was here to help," Brady agreed. "Although I wonder how this guy found you in the first place. You mentioned ditching Shelby's phone, so he must have somehow tracked her Jeep. We're going to leave that vehicle sitting in the parking lot for now. Follow me, I'll drive you both to the homestead so we can arrange for another ride."

"Wait, what?" Shelby scowled. "I can't just leave my car here."

"Yeah, you can." Aiden swallowed a wave of impatience. "I'll pay to have it towed back to your place. Which reminds me, I need to have my truck towed from the cemetery too. But later. Right now, we need to get out of here."

"That's ridiculous, it will cost a fortune." Shelby sighed, then relented. "Fine. But grab Eva's car seat."

"Will do." Brady waited for her to unlock the door so he could grab the car seat. "My vehicle is a half mile down the road."

"Would you like me to carry Eva?" He eyed Shelby as she hitched the toddler higher in her arms. The little girl was still sleeping and had to be like carrying deadweight.

"I'm okay." Her stubborn expression made him want to sigh. He took the canvas bag from her hand, realizing she'd packed Eva's clothes and toys.

"Please follow Brady. I'll walk behind you." As they set out down the road, he swept his gaze over the area, wondering exactly where the shooter had been standing. He needed to ask Gary to send him a copy of the video. Maybe there would be some way of identifying the gunman.

Brady unlocked his SUV, then took a minute to remove Caleb's booster seat to make room for Eva's car seat. When it was time to buckle Eva in, the little girl began to cry.

"Shh, it's okay. We're going for a ride. Here, would you like your dolly?" Shelby buckled the straps, then turned toward him. He quickly pulled out the cheap doll he'd purchased for Eva at the gas station, ridiculously pleased the little girl found comfort in the toy. "Here you go."

Eva clutched the doll close, then rested her cheek on the fake blond hair. Her eyes drifted shut.

Shelby crawled into the back seat on the other side, leaving him to sit up front with Brady. As they left the motel, he texted Gary about the video, then turned to Brady. "I don't feel right going to the homestead knowing Devon is still on bedrest. We're better off finding another motel."

Brady frowned. "Rhy wants you to stay until morning. It's not like you can get a rental at two in the morning. Even if the shooter tracked Shelby's Jeep, we should be safe enough at the homestead for a few hours."

He still didn't like bringing danger to his brother and his very pregnant wife, but he reluctantly nodded. No question he needed his siblings' help on this. Especially now that the shooter had found them at the American Lodge. "Okay. But only until morning. We'd appreciate a ride to the rental car agency."

"Not a problem." Brady turned and headed in the opposite direction. Aiden swiveled in his seat to look behind them.

"A tail?"

"Nope. Just making sure." Brady smiled. "It's become second nature to take the long route home."

"Yeah." Their family had been in many difficult situations over the past year. It was still difficult to comprehend that he'd been sucked into danger too. He hadn't gotten much sleep at the motel; his brain had worked overtime, ruminating over the shooting at Shelby's father's funeral, all the way back to Emmitt's death two years ago.

One or both of those situations had to be the root cause of this. Although he still couldn't quite understand why anything related to her husband and father would cause someone to target Emmitt's young widow and her daughter now.

After a solid twenty minutes, Brady pulled into the driveway of the homestead. The redbrick house with white trim and black shutters looked big from the outside. Not so much when they'd been younger and sharing bedrooms. There was only one low light on in the kitchen, and he knew Rhy and Devon always kept it on, as many of the siblings worked different shifts.

He and Elly were the only ones still living there. He'd saved up enough money to buy a house but hadn't taken the plunge. Mostly because he was at a crossroads with his career. Unsure which path to take.

"You grew up here?" Shelby asked, speaking for the first time during the drive. "It's an impressive home."

"Yeah." He pushed his door open. "There's plenty of spare bedrooms for us to use now that most of the siblings are married and living on their own. You won't feel crowded."

"That wasn't my concern." She yawned and began to unbuckle Eva's car seat. "It's just so different from what I'm used to."

Shelby grunted as she gathered Eva into her arms. He led the way up to the front door and entered the code to disarm the alarm system. He opened the door, then stepped back to let Shelby go inside first.

Brady followed him in, taking a moment to reset the alarm. Aiden shouldn't have been surprised to find Rhy sitting at the kitchen table, nursing a cup of coffee.

"Keep that up and you won't be able to sleep," Brady said.

"I'm not sleeping much anyway." Rhy raked his hand through his hair. "Devon needs her rest more than I do."

"These sleepless nights are practice for when the baby is born," Shelby said with a lopsided smile.

Rhy sighed. "I'm not sure if that's reassuring or frightening."

"Both," Aiden said. "Any preference as to which room Shelby and Eva use?"

"Take guest room closest to the bathroom." Rhy's expression softened when he eyed the toddler. "It's probably the most convenient."

"Understood. Shelby? This way . . ."

He thought she uttered a low groan upon seeing the curved staircase, but she carried Eva up one step at a time. Hovering in the doorway, he watched as she carefully placed her daughter in the bed.

The way she kissed Eva made his heart ache. Despite the way his siblings were all getting married and starting families, he hadn't spent much time thinking of having a family of his own. Well, until he'd gotten his paperwork to re-up for another tour in the National Guard.

Giving himself a mental shake, he turned away. He needed to talk through the plan with his brothers.

"Aiden? Wait." Shelby tucked Eva in, then hurried over. "Are you going back downstairs?"

"Yes. But you should try to get more rest."

"I'm coming with you." She brushed past him, to walk toward the curved staircase. "I want to hear what your brothers have to say."

"Let's go, then." He followed her down to the main level. Shelby was the one in danger; she deserved to have a say in their next move.

To a point.

"You really think Shelby's Jeep was tracked to the American Lodge?" Rhy was saying when they came in.

"Yes." Brady glanced at Shelby, then reluctantly added, "I didn't get a chance to check the vehicle for a GPS tracker. I'll do that tomorrow."

"A tracker?" Shelby looked alarmed. "Seriously?"

Brady shrugged. "You have a better idea on how you were found?"

Aiden mentally kicked himself for not considering that possibility before now. "Shelby's Jeep was at the cemetery. Easy enough for the shooter to have planted a tracking device while we were all at the grave site."

"But if there was a tracker, there was no reason to follow us on the interstate to my house."

"That's true. The shooter was waiting for us outside your home." He hated to admit the puzzle pieces didn't quite fit together. "Maybe they planned to make another attempt to shoot while we were driving."

"That's a risk," Rhy pointed out. "Shooting at a moving vehicle from another moving vehicle isn't as easy as it sounds."

"The shooter has missed twice now," Aiden agreed. "At the cemetery and at Shelby's house. If they had a tracker, why not wait until we were in the driveway and getting out of the vehicle?"

"Maybe they needed time to get away from the scene," Brady suggested.

"Maybe." Aiden wasn't convinced. "But anyone who'd been trained in the armed forces wouldn't botch their mission this badly."

"So maybe it's not a military guy," Rhy said.

"Or he hasn't served recently and has gotten rusty," Brady added. "The guy keeping an eye on the motel used military grade gear from what I could tell."

"That reminds me, Gary was going to send me the video." Aiden scrolled through his phone. The video wasn't as clear as he'd have liked, but a big part of that was the way the perp had stayed in the shadows of the trees. He played the short video but couldn't see anything remotely helpful.

"It's not much help." He quickly sent the video to his brothers, then catching Shelby's pointed look, handed his phone to her so she could see it too. "Do you recognize him?"

She stared intently at the screen. "No." She handed the phone back. "The goggles or binoculars cover most of his face."

"I'll send it to Ian, my tech guy," Brady said. "He might be able to clean it up a bit."

"We need a plan. Other than just getting a rental car." Aiden looked at his brothers expectantly.

"You mentioned your buddy in army intelligence," Rhy said. "Once you have a clean ride and a new place to stay, you should call him. Brady and I can do our best to keep digging for information too."

He couldn't come up with anything better, so he nodded. "Okay. That works. For now, we should get some sleep. Ready, Shelby?"

"Yes. Good night," Shelby said as she turned away.

"Good night," his brothers echoed.

He followed her upstairs, then gestured to the door to his room. "If you need anything, I'll be in here."

She nodded, then stared up at him. "I'm scared. It was one thing to have a gunman try to shoot me at the cemetery and my house, but to track me to the American Lodge? That seems so much more sinister."

He looped a friendly arm across her shoulders, giving her a brief hug. "We're safe here. And I promise I will always protect you and Eva."

"I know." She leaned against him for a moment. He would have liked to pull her closer still, but she abruptly broke away. "Good night."

"Good night." He stood in the hallway for a long moment after the door closed behind her. Shelby and Eva were safe here. But they couldn't run like this forever.

They needed to understand why Shelby had been targeted. And fast. Before another shooter managed to find them.

SHELBY DIDN'T THINK she'd fall asleep, but when Eva patted her cheek, she lifted her gritty eyelids, surprised to realize it was morning.

"I hav'ta go to the bathroom."

"Okay." She quickly slid out of the bed, hoping to get the little girl to the bathroom in time to avoid an accident. "This way."

"Where's the TV?" Eva looked around in confusion as Shelby hustled her daughter into the bathroom. "I wanna watch cartoons."

"We're visiting Mr. Aiden's house. I'm not sure where their TV is located." It wasn't that difficult to act as if nothing was wrong. She'd done the same thing after Emmitt's funeral. The fact that Eva hadn't even asked about her daddy had been telling. Then again, Eva had only been one year old when Emmitt had died. And it wasn't as if he'd been home a lot during the little girl's first year of life.

If Shelby was completely honest with herself, she had become so accustomed to Emmitt's long absences that she hadn't always missed him either. The silent acknowledgment brought a flash of guilt.

Why was she dredging all of this up now? There were bigger issues to be concerned about. Like the man with night-vision goggles who'd lurked outside her motel room. The one who may have placed a GPS tracker on her car.

"Here, let's wash our hands." She held Eva up to the sink to perform the task. When they emerged from the bathroom, she heard muted voices coming from the main level.

Noticing Aiden's door was open, she figured he was down there, likely with Brady and Rhy. Taking Eva's hand, she helped her daughter downstairs. The enticing scent of bacon and eggs wafted toward her.

She was surprised to find a pretty redhead cooking breakfast while Brady and Aiden sipped coffee. The woman's facial features resembled Aiden's, and she wasn't pregnant, so clearly this wasn't Devon.

"Oh, hi! You must be Shelby. And Eva too!" The redhead grinned widely. "I'm Elly. It's nice to meet you."

It took a moment for her to place the name. "You're the EMT, right?"

"That's right." Elly turned her attention to the stove. "Help yourself to some coffee. Breakfast will ready soon."

Shelby scowled at Aiden. "Shouldn't you be helping to make breakfast?"

Elly laughed. "He made the bacon. Don't worry, we all pitch in here."

"I'll get you some coffee," Aiden offered.

"Does Eva want milk?" Brady asked. He rose and went to the fridge. "Caleb is always hungry in the morning."

"Yes, thanks." She wasn't used to so many people crowding around so early in the morning. Sometimes even Eva's chattering was too much to handle before she'd had her morning hit of caffeine. She gratefully took the steaming mug from Aiden, watching with bemusement as Brady filled a small sippy cup with milk, then pulled a plastic booster seat from the pantry.

"Here you go, Eva." Brady lifted the little girl into the seat.

Her daughter reached for the sippy cup. "What do you say, Eva?"

"Thank you," Eva obediently responded.

"Rhy and Devon have already left for their early morning doctor's appointment." Aiden took the seat next to her. "Brady is going to take us to get a rental car after breakfast."

"Do you have to leave so soon?" Elly asked with a frown. "I miss having the siblings around."

"Don't worry, sis." Brady put his arm around Elly's shoulders. "Soon you'll have a new baby to help care for."

"I know, I really can't wait." Elly turned back to the stove. "Breakfast is ready."

Shelby sat beside her daughter while Aiden helped Elly bring the food to the table. Once they were seated, the

Finnegans all clasped their hands and bowed their heads. Brady led the prayer.

"Thank You for this food, Lord. And we also ask that You continue to keep Shelby and Eva safe in Your care. Amen."

"Amen," they all echoed.

"I've left a message for Tom Mitchell, my buddy who works in the Army Intelligence Office," Aiden said. "I'm hoping he'll call back soon."

"There are a few motels you can use to hide out," Brady said. "I asked Tarin about the safe house, but it's currently in use, although he's thinking it should be available in a day or two."

"A motel will be fine," Aiden said quickly.

Glancing at her daughter, she wished the safe house was an option, but she held her tongue. She trusted Aiden to keep them safe, regardless of where they stayed. "How is it that you know a guy in army intelligence?"

"I, uh"—Aiden looked flustered by the question—"I worked with him on a case once."

She sensed there was more to that story, but Aiden quickly stood and went to get the coffee carafe, refilling their cups. Then he went to work making another pot.

"I'm working through official channels for access to your father's military files," Brady said. "Your concern about a soldier who may have been dishonorably discharged is valid."

"Sounds good." She really did appreciate the Finnegan family chipping in to help.

Eva ate her scrambled eggs and bacon without complaint. When the little girl began to squirm in her seat, she lifted her out of the chair.

"Cartoons!" Eva said loudly.

"Here, I'll show you where they are." Brady jumped up to take her daughter into the living room.

"You can tell he's a father," she said, more to herself than anything.

"Yes, and a very good one." Elly smiled. "We were sad to have missed the early years with Caleb, but we're blessed to have him with us now."

"Why did you miss Caleb's early years?" Shelby asked.

"There isn't time to go through all the family stories," Aiden protested. "I can fill you in on Grace and Brady's path to finding each other later. We'll help clean the kitchen, then need to take off."

Elly looked disappointed but nodded. "I understand."

"Hey, why don't you pop in to visit Grace at her day care center?" Brady suggested upon returning to the kitchen. "She wouldn't mind a helping hand if you're off today. And that way you won't be here all alone."

"I will." Elly smiled. "I like helping in the infant room, and I don't work until this afternoon at three."

"Good idea." Aiden rose and carried his dishes to the sink. "I'll wash; Brady can dry."

"I'll dry." Shelby finished her last slice of bacon and went over to join him at the sink.

The camaraderie was nice. Maybe a bit overwhelming with so many people, but nice. Shelby was almost disappointed when it was time for them to go.

"I secured the rental for you under my name," Brady said as they headed out to his SUV. "And I also made a reservation for you at the Timberland Suites."

"Fancy," Aiden teased. "Why the special treatment?"

"Because Shelby and Eva deserve it." Brady grinned. "You're just along for the ride."

"Ha ha," Aiden muttered.

She couldn't help but smile. Once they were settled in the SUV, Brady backed out of the driveway. The neighborhood was nice, and from what she could tell, they were well outside the city limits.

She leaned forward. "How far to the car rental agency?"

"Ten minutes or so." Brady met her gaze in the rearview. "I rented a newer model Jeep SUV, similar to yours."

"Thanks." She settled back in her seat. "I hope Elly goes to visit your wife. I don't like thinking she might be in danger."

"Yeah." Aiden frowned. "Maybe she should have come with us."

"She'll be fine with Grace," Brady said. His phone rang, so he answered using the hands-free function. "What's up, Rhy?"

"Devon is being admitted to the hospital; they think she's in labor." Rhy's voice sounded tense. "I'm not worried, she's in good hands, but I tried to call Elly, she didn't answer."

"What?" Brady made a sharp right turn. "We're heading back to the homestead. I'm sure she's fine, but we'll check on her."

"Thanks. I'm probably overreacting," Rhy said. "But I appreciate you going over to make sure."

"It's fine. Keep us updated on Devon's progress," Aiden said. "And congrats, bro. You're going to be a father very soon."

"Thanks. Let me know when you reach Elly, okay?"

"Will do." Aiden and Brady exchanged concerned glances. "Later, Rhy."

A shiver of apprehension slid down her spine. She didn't want to believe the gunman had gone to the Finnegan homestead. But if he had? Elly was vulnerable there all alone.

Brady slowed a bit as they approached the Finnegan family home. The street was empty, and there were no cars on the driveway. She tried to relax but couldn't.

Brady stopped the SUV on the road in front of the house and put the gearshift in park. He turned to Aiden. "Get behind the wheel. You stay here to protect Shelby and Eva. I'll go inside to check Elly."

"Got it." Aiden pulled out his phone, then pushed his door open. "I'm calling for backup if I hear anything suspicious."

"Works for me." Brady slid out from behind the wheel and ran up to the front door of the house. Aiden climbed into the driver's seat.

They both watched as Brady took a moment to disarm the security system. She met Aiden's gaze in the rearview mirror and knew they shared the same thought. At least the system was still activated. If anyone had come here, they hadn't forced their way inside.

Then again, Elly seemed very friendly. It wasn't a stretch to believe Elly had invited the gunman inside.

The seconds ticked by so slowly she could hardly stand it. "What's taking him so long?"

Before Aiden could answer, she noticed a black SUV turning onto the street. As if in slow motion, she saw the vehicle speed up, turning so that they were heading straight toward them.

"Aiden!" She threw herself over Eva, bracing herself for the impact.

The crack of gunfire followed by shattering glass filled the air.

# CHAPTER FOUR

As Aiden fired two shots through the windshield, the driver of the oncoming vehicle abruptly swerved to avoid hitting them. Aiden aimed and fired a third time, determined to disable the vehicle, forcing the driver to stop. But it was no use. The vehicle careened out of sight.

"Shelby? Are you and Eva hurt?" He frantically twisted around to rake his gaze over them.

"I, uh, don't think so." Shelby's voice was muffled against her daughter's hair. His heart thundered in his chest, and he imagined she was even more frightened. She lifted her head to look at him. "How did they find us?"

"I don't know." He abruptly turned and pushed out of the vehicle, then reached for her door. "Come with me. We're going inside."

The faint wail of a siren indicated one or more of their neighbors had called the police to report shots fired. Not a normal occurrence in this area.

"Aiden! What happened?" Brady ran from the homestead, a confused Elly trailing behind him.

"Go back. Get inside." They were all vulnerable out here. Although he was glad Elly wasn't hurt. "Hurry!"

Elly spun around to do as he'd asked, but Brady continued toward them. His brother cranked open the rear passenger-side door to help get Eva and her car seat.

Aiden protected Shelby as much as possible as they scooted around the back of the vehicle toward the sidewalk leading to the front door of the house. When Shelby opened her arms for Eva, Brady shook his head. "No time. Move!"

Thankfully, Shelby didn't argue. In less than a minute, they were inside the homestead. Aiden took a moment to activate the security system, then turned to face his youngest sister. "Are you okay? Why didn't you answer your phone?"

"It was so weird," Elly said. "I kept getting static. I thought maybe the cellular carrier's service was down for some reason."

"Try it now," Brady said, handing Eva to Shelby.

Elly pulled out her phone. She scrolled through her contacts, then called Brady. When his brother's phone rang, she frowned. "It's working."

"Are you thinking what I'm thinking?" Aiden faced his brother. "Is it possible that SUV was using a signal jammer to prevent calls coming in or going out?"

"That's exactly what I'm thinking. They're relatively cheap to buy and work fairly well to interrupt communications." Brady blew out a breath. "Although there was no guarantee that we'd come back here. We could have sent one of our other siblings."

"Unless they've been watching the place." Aiden was overwhelmed with guilt at the expression of stark fear in Shelby's eyes. "Maybe they got here just as we were leaving and decided to use this tactic to force us to return."

"If so, their ruse worked like a charm." Shelby's voice trembled as she sank onto the sofa, still cradling Eva in her arms. "I thought for sure we were toast."

"I'm so sorry." He crossed over to pull her close. "I hate to admit I hadn't anticipated this."

"None of us did," Brady said calmly. "Not your fault."

It felt like it was his fault. He met Brady's gaze. "I shot up your windshield."

"All that matters is that everyone is safe and unharmed." Brady took the news in stride. It wasn't the first Finnegan vehicle to have suffered damage.

And likely wouldn't be the last.

"How are we going to get out of here?" Shelby asked.

"You should stay," Elly said. "All of you. We're safer here than anywhere else at the moment."

He met Brady's solemn gaze, a look of understanding passing between them. They weren't safe there. A brick building couldn't prevent the house from being peppered with bullets. Not when the bad guys knew they were there.

"We can't, El." He stood and crossed to his sister. "I'm sorry, but we need to get out of here ASAP."

"Why?" Elly looked bewildered.

"The shooter knows we're here." Brady spoke up, coming to his rescue. "Come on, sis. We'll take your car. It's been in the garage, so I'm hoping that will provide some desperately needed anonymity."

"Is there enough room for all of us?" Shelby asked.

"It will be tight, but we'll make it work." Aiden waved a hand at his sister. "Elly and Brady can drop us off at the rental car agency. Then they can head on to Grace's Bright Stars day care center."

Shelby nodded slowly. "Okay, that should work."

It had to work. He glanced at Brady. "Do we wait for the police to arrive?"

As if on cue, two Brookland squads pulled up near Brady's SUV. The officers slid out and eyed the bullet-ridden windshield.

"Guess so." Brady sighed and crossed to the door. "Elly, stay inside with Shelby and Eva. Aiden and I will handle this."

He gave his sister an encouraging smile. Elly quickly went over to sit beside Shelby and Eva. "Should we find cartoons?"

Leaving them inside alone wasn't easy, but he didn't think the shooter would return while cops were parked outside the house. Aiden stood beside Brady as his brother flashed his FBI creds.

It took longer than it should have to explain what had happened. When the officer wanted to take Aiden's gun for evidence, he reluctantly handed it over. Brady gave him an imperceptible nod, reassuring him that it was for the best.

Besides, he knew Rhy had a couple of additional hand-guns inside the gun safe. Not that he intended to let the Brookland cops know that.

"And you're sure you don't know who this guy is?" Officer Banfield pressed.

"I wish I did." Aiden met his gaze straight on. "Trust me, the sooner we identify this guy, the faster we'll be safe."

"You Finnegans are always in trouble," Banfield groused.

Since it was true, there was no point in arguing. And it wasn't like they went out looking for trouble.

Yet here they were, in the middle of a shootout in a nice, quiet, suburban neighborhood. Again. No wonder the Brookland cops were irked.

"Officer Banfield, would you mind escorting us to the car rental agency?" Brady smiled politely as he changed the subject. "Obviously, we can't drive the SUV, and we need a secure vehicle. Rhy is at the hospital with his wife. I know he'd appreciate you helping us out. We can take Elly's car, but we'd like to reach our destination without further mishap."

Aiden doubted the cops would agree, but the way Brady dropped Rhy's name was enough for Banfield to reluctantly nod. "Sure. We can do that."

"Thank you." He turned toward the front door, then glanced back over his shoulder. "Just give us a few minutes to get settled. Elly has a bright-blue SUV. We'll be out shortly."

"Okay," Banfield turned away. "Let's finish up with the photos."

He and Brady went back inside. He wasn't surprised to find Elly had a cartoon on a tablet she was showing to Eva. Even Shelby managed a wan smile.

"Everything okay?" Shelby asked.

"Yep. But we need to go." He took a moment to grab another weapon from Rhy's locked gun case. After holstering it and adding ammo, he reached for the car seat Brady had thought to bring inside. Then he swung a laptop computer case over his shoulder. "Elly, you have your keys handy?"

"I do." Elly pushed the tablet into Shelby's hands. "You should take this with you so you can keep Eva preoccupied."

"Oh, but . . ."

"I insist." Elly smiled. "You need it more than I do."

"Thanks, Elly." Shelby gave his sister an impulsive hug. "You're the best."

Brady had disarmed the security system and stood impatiently holding the door to the garage open. "We really need to go. The local cops are going to follow us to the rental car agency. Let's not keep them waiting."

Less than five minutes later, they were tucked like sardines in Elly's small SUV. As the women were smaller, they were tucked into the back next to Eva's car seat while he and Brady sat up front.

"We need to let Rhy know about this," Aiden said as Brady backed out of the driveway.

His brother waved at Officer Banfield, who slid into the driver's seat of his squad and began following them down the street. "Yeah, okay. Go ahead and call him. Make sure he knows everyone is safe and unharmed."

Aiden made the call. His oldest brother answered on the first ring. "You have Elly?"

"Yes. Everyone is safe. But we did run into some trouble." Aiden quickly explained what happened. "Brookland PD is giving us a personal escort to the rental agency. I grabbed the laptop off the desk too. Sorry."

"That's fine, I'm glad Brookland PD was there to help. But I don't like the sound of Elly's phone signal being jammed." Rhy sounded frustrated, probably because he wasn't there to take control of the situation the way he normally would. "I get that jammers aren't difficult to buy, but that was a level of technology I hadn't expected from this guy."

"I hear you." There were communication specialists in the army who were often deployed with them to various locations. Any soldier working alongside a communication specialist would know about signal jammers. He didn't think the knowledge helped them narrow down who was behind this.

"What about Elly?" Rhy demanded.

"Brady is going to drop Elly at Grace's day care center, then work on getting his SUV towed and repaired. He's also agreed to arrange for towing my truck and Shelby's Jeep." He shot his brother a sidelong glance. "We both agree we'll be safe once we're driving different vehicles."

"I hope so," Rhy muttered.

"How is Devon?" he asked. "And our future niece or nephew?"

"She's stable. The OB seems to think she'll deliver by the end of the day." Rhy sounded happy about that. "Speaking of which, I need to go. Be safe, okay? And keep me updated."

"We will, don't worry. Just focus on taking care of your wife and baby. Oh, and give Devon a hug from us."

"Will do." Rhy ended the call.

Aiden lowered his phone, then frowned. "You don't think the gunmen could have tracked my phone, do you?"

"Maybe." Brady shrugged. "They seem awfully determined."

"They?" Elly echoed. "You mean there are more than one of them?"

"Not necessarily," he hastened to assure her. He opened his window and tossed the phone out, listening to it shatter on the concrete. "We believe it's just one gunman, but we honestly don't know for sure."

"Gu-man?" Eva echoed.

The little girl's innocent question was like a dropkick to the center of his chest. He turned to see Shelby's stricken gaze. "What's your dolly's name?"

"Dolly!" Eva held up the plastic doll.

"She calls all of them Dolly," Shelby explained with a

strained smile. "I think she gets that from her preschool program."

"Well, your dolly is beautiful." Aiden racked his brain for something else to say. "Do you have a favorite color? Mine is blue."

"Pink." Eva didn't hesitate, and he was impressed when she pointed to Dolly's pink dress. "My faborite."

"Favorite," Shelby corrected gently. She looked relieved that Eva seemed to have forgotten about the gunman.

No three-year-old should have to be afraid of gunmen. Aiden swallowed a flash of rage at whoever was behind this. No matter what Shelby's father had done, taking out an innocent woman and child was unacceptable.

"The rental agency is up ahead." Brady's comment snagged his attention. "Don't forget, I secured a room at the Timberland Falls Suites."

"I remember." It seemed like hours ago that they'd had that conversation. When Brady pulled into the parking lot, the Brookland squad car followed. Officer Banfield waved as he got out and helped unbuckle Eva's car seat. He carried the car seat and computer while Eva walked into the building beside her mother.

Inside the rental agency, it only took a minute for him to get the key for a newer model Jeep SUV. It was green in color, and while he'd have preferred black to blend in with the night, he didn't protest.

"I hope this works," Shelby said, once they were settled inside. "I can't take much more of this."

"It will." He hated seeing her so dejected. "We don't have my phone, and we have a clean car. We're good to go from here."

Shelby stared at him for a moment, then turned to gaze out the window. He winced, understanding her concern. Based on everything that had happened in what, less than twenty-four hours? The danger had been relentless.

He wanted to reassure her but couldn't. Not when he had no idea who was doing this or why.

All he could offer was a temporary reprieve. And pray that it was enough.

---

SHELBY'S ANGER simmered at a low boil. Sure, she knew this mess wasn't Aiden's fault. Yet just hearing Eva cry and then mention the word gunman had been like a sucker punch. She hated everything about her baby being in danger. Wasn't it bad enough that her daughter had lost her father, then her pappa? Did she have to be targeted by gunfire too?

*Why, Lord, why?*

Her silent plea went unanswered.

"Shelby?" Aiden's low voice didn't offer any comfort. Yet she did her best to let go of her fury, long enough to glance at him.

"What?" She softened her tone. "I'm sorry. I wasn't paying attention."

"The units at Timberland Falls have small kitchens. Should we stop to get some groceries?"

"Is it safe?" The question came out harsher than she'd intended.

"Good point. We'll order groceries to be delivered." Aiden didn't take offense at her comment, which only made her feel worse. "I thought it would be easier to have snacks brought in for Eva."

He was trying so hard. She swallowed her ire and

nodded. "Yes, it would. Thanks for thinking of that. Ordering groceries is a great idea."

"I'm glad." He eyed her warily. "I'm going to call Tom again once we're settled. I need his help to move forward on this."

At the mention of his buddy in army intelligence, she shrugged. "I hope he answers. I can't put my life on hold forever."

"I understand. Trust me, I want this over as much as you do."

"I do trust you." She managed a smile. "I'm truly grateful for everything you've done. Your family, too, for that matter. Elly is a sweetheart."

"That she is," Aiden agreed.

She noticed he watched the rearview mirror frequently during their trip to Timberland Falls. She appreciated his determination and tenacity, yet no matter what tactics they'd used, the bad guy had still found them.

Because his phone had been tracked? Or by some other method? She wasn't the most tech-savvy person on the planet. She hadn't realized that there were devices out there that jammed electronic signals. Yet the Finnegans had seemed to be aware of that possibility.

Twenty minutes later, Aiden pulled into the parking lot of the hotel. It was nice, at least from the outside. Likely more expensive compared to the American Lodge.

Eva was just starting to get antsy. After unbuckling her daughter from her car seat, Eva pushed at her.

"I wanna walk."

"Okay, but take my hand." She captured her hand. Eva held it for a moment before pulling away and running toward the building. Shelby couldn't blame the little girl for needing to burn off some youthful energy.

"Look out," Aiden warned, carrying the computer case and plastic bag of items his family had been kind enough to give them, including the tablet. "There might be cars."

Shelby hurried to catch up, quickly opening the door for Eva. Her daughter skipped inside, swinging her dolly from one hand. "What's this place, Mommy?"

"A hotel." Shelby smiled as Eva swung in a circle, looking around curiously. Her daughter's favorite questions these days were centered on the words *What's that?* and *Why?*

"Are we gonna live here?" Eva asked.

"No, this is just a little vacation. Come with me now. We have to wait for Mr. Aiden to check us in."

Aiden already had the room key cards in hand. He politely thanked the desk clerk, then turned and led the way down the hall. "We have a suite on the first floor."

She wondered if he'd requested that on purpose. Or if Brady had.

They passed a pool, which caught Eva's eye. "Swim! I wanna swim!"

"We will, later." She didn't have a swimming suit for the girl but could possibly make do with a T-shirt and shorts. "If you're good."

"I'm always good." Eva pouted, then said, "I wanna swim *now*."

Under normal circumstances, she might have stood her ground. But they'd been moving from place to place since leaving the funeral yesterday. And really, swimming was likely the best way to distract the little girl from the danger. "Soon, Eva."

"Do we need to order more clothes?" Aiden asked as he unlocked the room to their suite. She followed him across the threshold, impressed at the size of the room.

"Getting a couple of swimsuits for me and Eva would be nice." She grimaced. "I understand that's not a priority, though."

"We'll get what you need." He set the computer bag on the table, then handed her the clothes his family had gotten. He smiled at the little girl. "Eva deserves to have fun."

She put a hand on his arm. "Thank you."

"It's the least I can do." He gestured to the desk. "Make a list for me, okay?" He pulled out the two disposable phones his brother had purchased. He handed one to her. "Keep this with you. I've programmed my number so you can call me if needed."

"Thanks."

He turned on the computer, did a quick search, then stood. "Excuse me for a minute as I follow up with Tom."

"Sure." She glanced at her daughter. "Do you want to watch cartoons while we wait for our swimming suits?"

"Yes!" Eva hopped from one foot to the other. "I want pink."

She always did. Shelby turned on the television, then went to make a list. Before she'd finished, Aiden came over.

"I'll put the order in, but Tom Mitchell is already in town." His gaze was serious. "We may have to wait until after we talk to him to go to the pool."

"That's okay." She nodded to where Eva was watching television. "That will hold her attention for a while. And I have no idea how long it takes for clothing and grocery items to be delivered."

Aiden held her gaze. "Tom is keenly interested in talking to you, Shelby. You'll need to be here for the interview."

"Me?" She stared. "Why?"

"I assume he may have already uncovered some information that he needs verified."

"About my father?" Her stomach clenched. "Nothing bad, I hope."

"He wouldn't go into detail. But he'll be here in thirty minutes." Aiden peered at the list from his position over her shoulder. "Are you sure there's nothing else you need?"

"This should do it." She felt bad asking for extras like swimming suits and flotation toys. But now that Eva had seen the pool for herself, there was no getting around letting her swim. "Thanks again."

He nodded and crossed to the corner of the sofa to place the order. When he finished, he glanced up. "They'll deliver in an hour."

"Wonderful." She should be able to hold Eva off that long.

She took a moment to check out the bedrooms, deciding on the room that held two twin beds. Each room had their own bathroom, which was another luxury.

Maybe it was time for her to view this as a mini vacation. Stressing about the gunman finding them again wasn't helpful. And she didn't want Eva to pick up on her concern. Kids could be perceptive about their parents' emotions.

Twenty-five minutes later, Aiden's disposable cell rang. After glancing at the screen, he answered. "Where are you?"

She watched as Aiden strode to the door. "Come straight down the hall on the right from the lobby. We're in suite 1117."

Her belly fluttered with nervousness. Why, she wasn't sure. In a way, learning her father had been involved in something that had sent this gunman after her, would be a blessing. At least they'd know who to track down and arrest.

That had to be better than living in limbo, waiting for the next strike.

"Staff Sergeant Finnegan." The soldier at the door was dressed in camouflage fatigues rather than dress blues. He held out his hand. "I'm Lieutenant Tom Mitchell."

"Please, call me Aiden." He shook his hand, then stepped back to let the guy in. "This is Mrs. Shelby Copeland and her daughter, Eva."

"Mrs. Copeland." Lieutenant Mitchell was all about formality. "Please accept my sincere condolences on your loss."

"Thank you." She rose to shake his hand. "We appreciate your help in finding out who has been shooting at me."

"Yes, ma'am." Mitchell glanced at Eva, then at Aiden. "Is there a place we can speak privately?"

"I'm afraid this is as private as it gets." She gestured to the table in the small kitchenette. "Let's sit down. I doubt Eva will pay any attention to our adult conversation."

The somber expression on Mitchell's face was not the least bit reassuring. Feeling as if he was about to give bad news, she sank into the closest chair and clasped her hands together to keep them from trembling.

"We've been shot at three times now." Aiden dropped beside her. "You may as well tell us what you know."

Mitchell nodded. "You remember I was assigned to investigate Sergeant Copeland's death."

She sucked in a harsh breath, glancing sharply at Aiden. This was news to her.

"Yes. But you deemed the incident an accident." Aiden frowned. "No foul play."

"That is what I told you," Mitchell said with a nod. "However, there were some rumblings among the enlisted men about Sergeant Copeland. Those notes are still on file and may impact what is happening today."

"How?" She forced the word through her constricted throat. "Tell me how this is related to my deceased husband."

Mitchell hesitated. "There was a rumor about an affair between Sergeant Copeland and a female sergeant."

"An affair?" She stared at him blankly. "You mean, an extramarital affair?"

"Yes, I'm afraid so." Mitchell seemed to look toward Aiden for support. "I'm here to find out what, if anything, you know about that."

She had to curl her fingers into fists. "Nothing." She shook her head. "I know nothing, and even more? I refuse to believe a word of this nonsense." She rose and stumbled from the living area, seeking refuge in the bedroom.

But the officer's words continued to reverberate through her head.

*Affair. Affair. Affair.*

She buried her face in her hands, stifling the urge to cry. She didn't want to believe it. But if it was true? Emmitt had betrayed her in the worst way possible.

# CHAPTER FIVE

"We shouldn't have dropped the news on her like that. She clearly had no idea her husband may have cheated on her." Aiden was torn between learning more about Mitchell's investigation and rushing over to comfort Shelby.

Not that she'd want to be comforted by him.

"I feel bad about that," Mitchell admitted. "But if the rumors of an affair are true, then it could be related to the shooting attempts."

He glanced over to make sure Eva was still focused on the cartoon. "I knew Emmitt, not really well, but we were acquaintances. I never heard the rumors of an affair."

"Rumor isn't fact," Mitchell said. "I didn't find any proof of the liaison."

"Two years have passed since Copeland's death. Why would anyone bother to come after his widow and daughter now?"

"I have a theory." Mitchell hesitated, then said, "What if Shelby's father learned of the affair? And took action against the female sergeant involved?"

He frowned. "I see your point. But Sergeant Major

Savage died of a heart attack. Even if he had uncovered something, there's no reason to come after Shelby and her daughter now."

"You asked for insight." Mitchell shrugged. "It's only rumor and theory, but if the sergeant major had taken action, that may have been the impetus to lash out against Shelby."

"Do you have a name of the female sergeant?" He had trouble wrapping his mind around this. "An interview with her would clear this up, so we can move on to another theory."

"Unfortunately, I don't. I told you, there was no proof that Copeland was involved with anyone. However, hearing about the recent shooting attempts made me wonder if we missed something when we investigated his death two years ago."

He swallowed a flash of frustration. "Is there a way to see if Savage did take action against a female sergeant? That may be a place to start."

"Working on that." Mitchell grimaced. "You know how the army is, though. They haven't been very transparent with information."

Would Brady run into the same roadblock? Probably. If the army wouldn't cooperate with their own investigator, he doubted they'd open their files to the feds. "We need to know who Copeland had an affair with."

Mitchell reached into his soft-sided computer case and withdrew a sheet of paper. "I ran a list of all female personnel serving in the National Guard. I didn't limit the list to those of higher rank because I didn't want to miss anyone. And again, the rank of sergeant was a rumor. Could be he had a relationship with an enlisted soldier."

"That would definitely get the sergeant major's attention; superiors are not allowed to date subordinates, much less have affairs with them." He took the list, running his gaze down the list of names. "Twenty-five women." He glanced up at Mitchell. "I expected more."

"I only ran the names of those who served in this area." The investigator shrugged. "It doesn't seem likely he'd have time to meet up with a woman stationed on the East or West Coast."

"I get it, but what if the woman involved has since left the army?"

"I ran a quick check on that, too, and added three names." Mitchell leaned forward to point to the bottom of the list. "These names marked with an asterisk were working here but left within the last two years."

"We should start with those three women first. Although maybe we should go back even farther than that." Aiden couldn't help but feel a surge of satisfaction to have something to focus on. "It makes sense that a female soldier would want a fresh start elsewhere after the man you were having a secret affair with died in the line of duty. Maybe the woman in question broke things off ahead of his death."

"True." Mitchell sighed. "But this is only one theory, Finnegan. I could be way off base here. For all I know, there's someone from Ms. Copeland's past who has decided to come after her."

"Yeah." Aiden set the paper down on the desk. "She's a schoolteacher. Hard to imagine she has enemies."

"Her father could have many enemies," Mitchell said. "Someone with a grudge and mentally imbalanced could think that killing her will even the score."

It was difficult to imagine anyone taking their anger to that extent. Lashing out at the sergeant major was one thing, but an innocent woman and her child? Incomprehensible.

Yet he had seen some mentally unstable people during the course of his deployments. Especially those involved in moblike activity. It didn't take long for a routine protest to turn ugly. No matter which side of the political aisle was involved.

He focused on the issue at hand. "Any way to identify who had been disciplined by Shelby's father?"

"I'm working on that." Mitchell looked as frustrated as Aiden felt. "I'm waiting for the upper brass to approve my request."

He had to bite back an angry retort. Someone had taken shots at Shelby three times in less than twenty-four hours! They didn't have time. They needed answers now.

The bedroom door opened. Shelby stepped out, her face puffy from crying. She avoided his gaze, walking over to sit beside her daughter.

"When can we swim?" Eva asked.

"Soon." Shelby's smile was strained. "We're waiting for our swimsuits to arrive, remember?"

"Don't wanna swim *soon*. I wanna swim *now*." Eva's insistent tone made him smile. But Shelby only appeared more stressed.

"If you don't behave, we won't swim at all." Shelby's sharp tone startled him, but then she gestured toward the television and added, "Be a good girl, Eva. Keep watching your show."

Eva lapsed into silence as her attention was once again riveted by the cartoon. Watching the interaction gave him a new appreciation for all parents. Especially single mothers. Being a parent was a full-time job.

"I wish I had more information to share," Mitchell said in a low voice. Likely trying to avoid Shelby overhearing.

"It's fine. But I need you to keep me informed on your progress." Aiden frowned. "You need to make it clear to the bars and stars how much danger Shelby and her daughter are in."

Bars and stars was slang for upper brass. As a staff sergeant, Aiden had bars on his sleeve, but he was nowhere near the level of making big decisions.

"I will. I'll give them the details on this latest attempt. Maybe that will spur them into moving faster."

It shouldn't take blazing guns for that, but Aiden nodded. "I'd appreciate it."

Surprisingly, Shelby stood and came back to the table, pinning Mitchell with a stern gaze. "Do you have proof?"

"No, ma'am. I don't." Mitchell lifted his chin. "As I said, there were rumors. I was hoping you'd know something that might help us."

A myriad of expressions contorted her features. Anger, confusion, stubbornness, then finally acceptance. "I didn't know about the affair. That came as a complete shock. But I can admit that things were somewhat strained between us."

That information hit Aiden in the chest like a brick. "What do you mean?"

She huffed. "You haven't been married, so maybe you don't understand. It's not all sunshine and roses. We had our fights. Especially after Eva was born. He refused to take a leave of absence to be home with me." With a glance toward Eva, she added, "With us. Now I have to wonder if that was because of this other woman rather than his commitment to the army."

"You're right, I haven't been married. And I can appreciate a relationship takes work. On both sides." His older siblings made it look easy, but he knew there was a lot of compromise involved. "I'm sorry to hear things had been a little rocky."

"I'm surprised you didn't know about his cheating." She narrowed her eyes. "I thought you were his friend."

"I wasn't as close to him as some of the other guys, and unfortunately, I was busy with my own team of soldiers." But her comment did make him think. He turned toward Mitchell. "We need to interview Emmitt's close friends. They would be more likely to know about his indiscretions."

"They denied that two years ago." Mitchell slowly nodded. "But you're right. Now that Emmitt's widow and child are in danger, they may be more likely to talk."

"Both Oliver Kennedy and Victor Morrison were at the cemetery. Maybe start with them." Aiden wished he could accompany the investigator to interview the men, but he would not leave Shelby and Eva alone. Or drag them from one place to the other. "I'm sure they'll give you some insight into whatever was going on with Emmitt before he died."

"I will." Mitchell turned a solemn gaze toward Shelby. "Ms. Copeland, I'm truly sorry to be the bearer of bad news."

Shelby stared at her hand, then shrugged. "It's okay. I'll get over it." Then she scowled. "But if you discover there is no truth to this rumor, I hope you make sure my husband's name is cleared. I don't want anyone thinking badly of him if it's not warranted." Her voice hitched. "He served his country well. I don't want his memory tarnished for no reason."

"I promise." Mitchell rose. He held out his hand, and Shelby took it. "I'm sorry for your loss. Thanks again for meeting with me."

"Of course. Thank you for coming." Shelby's voice was subdued.

"Make a note of my new cell number." Aiden rattled it off, then made a point of adding Tom's name to his cheap disposable phone. "I have a computer, so I can start digging into the list of names as soon as possible."

"Good. I'll keep hounding the upper brass." Mitchell nodded thoughtfully. "Between the two of us, we should be able to make progress."

He followed Mitchell to the door. After the intelligence officer left, he turned to find Shelby reading the list of female soldiers. He wished more than anything he could spare her this pain. Hadn't she already suffered enough?

Yet she could be right about this being nothing more than a nasty rumor. His brother Tarin often mentioned how the search for truth could be messy. Ripping open people's personal lives revealed secrets better left buried.

He had a very bad feeling that this was exactly what would happen here.

A call on the hotel room phone startled him. He reached across the desk to pick up the receiver. "Hello?"

"Your delivery is here." He recognized the voice of the front desk clerk who had checked him in.

"Thanks, I'm coming." He hung up, then glanced at Shelby. "Food and swimming gear has arrived. I'll be right back."

"Great." She pushed the list of names aside; although from the furrow in her brow, he knew she understood the significance of the information. All possible names of the woman Emmitt had cheated on her with.

Picking up the supplies didn't take long. Aiden had his hands full, though, so he had to use his elbow to knock on the door. A moment later, Shelby swung the door open. He hoped she'd checked the peephole first.

"Thanks." He set the items on the desk.

Eva bounced on the sofa with excitement. "Time to swim! Time to swim!"

He chuckled at her enthusiasm. "Take the clothes." He handed that bag over. "I'll put the food away while you change."

Shelby managed a small smile, then turned to her daughter. "Come with me, Eva."

He quickly unpacked the snacks, then set about blowing up the water wings and beach ball Shelby had requested.

When the two of them emerged from the bedroom, he tried not to swallow his tongue. Shelby wore a conservative blue one-piece that favored her eyes. She was stunning, and Eva was cute wearing her frilly pink swimming suit. They both carried towels from the bathroom. Shelby wrapped hers around her waist.

He handed her the beach ball, then bent to slip Eva's arms through the water wings. "Ready to go?"

"Aren't you swimming too?" Eva cocked her head curiously.

"Not today." He smiled and reached for the door. He met Shelby's gaze, and added, "I'll watch."

"Okay!" Eva wasn't deterred. She ran down the hall toward the pool, leaving him and Shelby to follow more slowly.

"You should have ordered swimming trunks too." She shifted the ball to one arm so she could unlock the door to the indoor pool.

"I'd rather be on lifeguard duty." He spoke lightly, but in reality, he took his role as protector seriously.

Watching Shelby and Eva playing in the pool made him smile. The moment of normalcy was at odds with the threat that lurked outside the hotel.

And he silently vowed to find the person responsible before the gunmen struck again.

---

SHELBY WAS KEENLY aware of Aiden watching from the side of the pool. Dealing with Eva made it impossible to hold on to her anger.

Emmitt had cheated. Seeing the list of women's names had hit hard. One of them was likely the adulteress.

She told herself it didn't matter. Emmitt was gone. But her stomach churned with the knowledge that she'd been so foolish, naïve, and gullible. Believing that Emmitt had been a dedicated husband and father, determined to protect and serve his country.

When in reality he'd been sleeping with another woman.

No proof, Tom Mitchell had said. But deep down she knew it was true. In a way, it explained the distance she'd felt growing between them in the months prior to Emmitt's death.

A wave of nausea hit hard, and she had to swallow to keep from throwing up. Emmitt's betrayal wasn't important. Keeping her daughter safe was.

And if that meant digging up the truth, then so be it.

"Mommy, look! I'm swimming!" Eva stood on the bottom of the shallow section of the pool, slapping her arms on the water, splashing herself in the face. She smiled, then swam over to join her.

"Like this." She lifted Eva so she was lying on her

tummy, then gently drew her through the water. The water wings helped keep Eva's face above the water, and it occurred to her that she should enroll the little girl in swimming lessons.

Maybe once this nightmare was over.

Eva splashed and played, enjoying herself immensely. Soon, the heaviness in her chest lightened.

It was hard to grieve for something that had taken place a long time ago when her daughter needed her. Eva was the most important person in her life.

Shelby would do anything to protect the little girl.

After forty-five minutes, she carried Eva from the pool. "Time to get dressed."

"Nooo," Eva wailed. "I wanna swim!"

"Maybe later." She had sensed Aiden getting antsy, although he hadn't said anything. "Look, our fingers are wrinkly. Time to take a break."

Eva stared at her fingertips with fascination. "Will the wrinkles go away?"

"Yes, very soon." She draped a towel around the little girl. "Let's go back to the room."

Eva reluctantly allowed her to take her hand so they could head back to the room.

"Thanks." Shelby smiled at Aiden. "I know this wasn't easy for you, but Eva enjoyed herself."

"Of course." His deep husky voice made her shiver. Or maybe she was feeling the chill from the cold air in the hallway. Yeah, that was it. She wasn't interested in Aiden. She wasn't interested in anyone. "You and Eva deserve some fun."

She nodded, then waited for him to use the room key to get back into their suite. Steering Eva toward the bedroom, she said, "We'll need to think about lunch."

"We'll order room service when you're finished," Aiden said.

She nodded and closed the door. It took longer than she'd have liked to strip off their wet things, shower, and change into dry clothes. Eva squirmed as she tried to brush her damp hair.

"No, Mommy." Eva ducked to avoid the grooming. "I wanna watch TV."

"Not until after lunch. Now hold still." She managed to drag a brush through her daughter's blond tresses enough to get rid of most of the tangles. Then she stepped back to tend to her own hair.

Eva ran out of the room. Lowering the brush, she stared at her reflection for a moment. She wasn't beautiful, but Emmitt had seemed enamored of her when they'd first met, sweeping her off her feet in a whirlwind romance. When had things changed? After Eva had been born? Or even before that?

What had caused him to look at her and find her lacking? Had she done something that had sent him into the arms of another woman?

*Stop it.* She pushed the wave of self-doubt aside. Emmitt's cheating wasn't her fault. It was his.

And now, it was also hers. If that indiscretion had indeed set this terrifying string of events into motion.

She and Eva did not deserve this.

Anger helped keep her steady. She used the blow-dryer, then went to join Aiden and Eva.

"What do you like to eat?" Aiden was asking. "Chicken tenders?"

"Yes! Tenders!" Eva bounced up and down on the chair. "With ketchup."

"Sounds good." Aiden met her gaze. "Uh, if that's okay with your mom."

"It's fine." She cocked her head, regarding him thoughtfully. "I'm surprised you know what kids like to eat."

"Learned everything I know from Brady's son, Caleb. He's six and as full of unlimited energy as Eva." He grinned. "I have less practice with women. What would you like? It's not an extensive menu, I'm afraid."

She crossed over to see for herself. "The chicken ranch wrap is fine. Thanks."

While Aiden placed their order, she went over to turn the TV off.

"Mommy," Eva protested.

"After lunch." She gave the little girl a stern look. "We don't eat in front of the TV."

Their room service meal arrived quicker than she'd anticipated. The pool had been empty, so maybe they weren't very busy today.

Aiden unpacked their meals. Then he reached out to take her hand. "I'll say grace."

Surprised, she nodded and bowed her head.

"Dear Lord Jesus, we thank You for this food and for continuing to keep us safe in Your care. Amen."

"Amen." She lifted her head. "Do all the Finnegans pray?"

"Yes." He grinned. "Oh, we tried to rebel after our parents died, eleven years ago now. But Rhy and Tarin were not having it. They stepped in to raise us and insisted we continue practicing our faith. Looking back, I think that was a big reason why we stayed so close."

"Your family is amazing." She was impressed at how the siblings had stuck together through such a difficult time. "I didn't realize you lost your parents so young."

"Yeah, it wasn't easy. But things would have been much worse if not for Rhy and Tarin." He grinned. "Alanna and I tried to get away with stuff, but they seemed to anticipate every move we made."

"They were young once too," she pointed out.

"That's exactly what Rhy said. He told us he and Tarin had done everything we'd tried, and some stuff we hadn't even thought of."

That made her laugh. "I bet that made you both try to come up with new ideas."

"We did." Aiden flashed a smile. "But then we had college prepare for and Elly to protect." His humor faded. "She's been doing great in her role as an EMT. But I can't shake the idea that she doesn't love her job."

"Does anyone?" She flushed, then said, "I mean, yes, I enjoy being a teacher, but that doesn't mean I come home each day raving about how great it is. Every job has challenges."

"That might be it." He shrugged, took a bite of his burger, then said, "We talked about placing bets on how long Elly would last, but Rhy shut that down. I guess we'll just wait and see."

It was easy to see that the siblings had a soft spot for the youngest Finnegan. Being an only child, she'd never experienced the camaraderie he'd described.

Glancing at Eva, happily munching her chicken nuggets, she realized her daughter would be an only child too.

Not something she'd planned. It hurt to think back to how she and Emmitt had discussed having several children.

They ate in silence for a few minutes. Her gaze rested on the list of female soldiers. "How do you plan to investigate them? Do you have access to army records?"

"No, but I can try social media." Aiden frowned. "Do you have an account?"

She shook her head. "No, I did for a while but shut it down after Eva was born. I found there were too many creeps on there."

"True," Aiden said. "Our family isn't big into social media either, especially my cop siblings. It was never a thing in our house, but some people are really active, so it's worth a try."

She couldn't argue his logic. She knew several of her colleagues were constantly posting stuff. Her cheeks burned as she considered the possibility that the woman who'd had an affair with Emmitt had pictures of the two of them together posted online.

"I'm done, Mommy." Eva swiped at her face, smearing ketchup across her cheek. "Can I watch TV now?"

"Okay, just a minute." She wet a napkin to clean Eva's face and hands. Then she stood and turned the television back on.

Returning to her seat, she picked up the last of her wrap. Funny, an hour ago she'd wanted to throw up. Now she was finishing lunch.

"Hey." Aiden reached over to take her hand. "I'm really sorry. I wish we could have saved you the stress of hearing all of this."

"Yeah, well, you're not responsible for Emmitt's actions." She held his hand, grateful for the connection. "And it's worth the agony if we can figure out who is responsible. Eva doesn't deserve this."

"Neither do you." Aiden shocked her by picking up her hand and kissing it. "You're an amazing woman, Shelby."

She didn't feel amazing. Although Aiden's warm brown

gaze did make her feel special. Before she could say anything more, his cell phone rang.

He squeezed her hand, then reached for the phone. "It's Tom Mitchell," he said, before answering. "Hey, Tom, what's up?"

She couldn't hear the other side of the conversation, but Aiden only listened for a moment before lowering the phone. He lurched to his feet. "We have to go."

"What? Go where?"

"Away from here." He tossed the computer into the bag, then reached for her hand. "Get Eva's coat. Hurry."

"What's going on?" She reached for their coats.

"Tom's injured." His gaze darkened. "He thinks the shooter has found him."

# CHAPTER SIX

The agonized whisper from Tom Mitchell indicating he was struck by random gunfire was all the warning he'd needed. In that moment, Aiden knew Mitchell had been followed.

Their location was compromised. They needed a new plan, fast!

Shoving the list of names into the computer case, he threw the strap over his shoulder. Then he quickly tossed Eva's toys and some snacks into another bag. While he was doing that, Shelby managed to get Eva's coat on, then shrugged into her own. He ushered them out of the room and down the long hallway to the lobby.

"Stay behind me." He rested his right hand on his weapon as he peered through the glass door. There was nothing suspicious in the lobby area, so he pushed through the door.

He'd left their rental SUV in a parking spot located near the front door. Now he wished he'd parked in a different location, somewhere less noticeable. Glancing over his shoulder, he met Shelby's frightened gaze.

"I need you and Eva to get into the Jeep ASAP," he whispered. "Don't worry about belting her in until we're on the road."

She gave a jerky nod. He was all for safety, but there wasn't time to waste. He worried they'd taken too long to get their stuff already.

"Now." He shoved the door open and led the way outside. Shelby and Eva crowded close. He waited for them to scramble into the back seat before sliding in behind the wheel. He started the engine, then shifted into reverse. He was out of the parking spot and out onto the road in less than ten seconds.

"Get into your car seat," Shelby said. "I'll buckle you in."

"What about my cartoons?" Sparing a glance at the rearview mirror, he was relieved Eva seemed oblivious to the danger. "I wanna finish my show."

"We'll watch something on Elly's tablet." Shelby's voice was calm, but her wide eyes and pale skin betrayed her fear. He desperately wished he'd considered the possibility of Tom being followed.

Yet he found it strange that the investigator had been targeted. If the gunman truly wanted Shelby and Eva, why not wait outside the hotel? Why follow Tom and then take a shot at him?

To flush them out of hiding? He tightened his grip on the steering wheel, feeling as if he'd walked right into their trap.

Swallowing hard, he took a winding path around the Timberland Falls Suites before heading for the interstate. Instead of driving south toward Brookland, he turned west. It was pretty much the only option. They'd come from the south. Shelby's house was north. There wasn't enough terrain between their current location and the eastern shore of Lake Michigan.

Would the shooter come to the same conclusion? He didn't know.

*Help us, Lord! Guide us to safety!*

The whispered prayer didn't ease his concerns. The road heading west ended up being far more twisty and curvier than he'd anticipated. Those moments where he couldn't see the road behind him ratcheted his tension up several notches.

He took a moment to pull his disposable cell phone from his pocket. He handed it over the console to Shelby. "I need you to call my brother Brady."

She took the phone. "What should I tell him?"

"We need a safe house ASAP." He hit the brakes as another hairpin curve loomed up ahead. "Put the call on speaker. I'll explain what little I know."

"Okay." There was a moment of silence before she spoke. "Brady? This is Shelby, I'm putting this on speaker so Aiden can talk to you." She did so and held the phone between them. "Go ahead, Aiden."

"Army Investigator Tom Mitchell has been shot roughly ninety minutes after we met with him at the hotel. He managed to call and warn me, so we left Timberland Falls." He gave the SUV more gas, thankful there was a straight stretch of highway ahead of him. "We need a safe house, something that can't be traced back to the family."

"Okay, give me a few minutes. I'll talk to Tarin too." Brady paused, then said, "You're not hurt? Everyone's okay?"

"Yes." But for how much longer? Hiding from an unknown perp was taking a toll on Shelby and Eva.

"Where are you now?" Brady asked.

"We're on Highway 175 heading northwest." There were several cars behind them, but he couldn't tell if one of them was a tail. "I'm honestly not sure which way to go."

"Stay the course," Brady advised. "I'll call you back in five minutes."

"Thanks." He tried to relax his deathlike grip on the steering wheel.

"I can't believe Tom was hurt." Shelby's voice wobbled. "All because he tried to help us."

"I feel bad about the situation too." He briefly met her gaze in the rearview mirror. "But we didn't start this. The shooter did. The attempt to take Tom Mitchell out of the picture tells me we're getting close to the truth. Whoever is behind this must have army training at the very least. He or she may even still wear the uniform."

"You really think the shooter could be a woman?" She hesitated, then added, "Maybe even the same one who had the affair with Emmitt?"

"Maybe." He believed anything was possible. His sister Kyleigh was an expert marksman, no reason one of the female soldiers couldn't do the same. "The bad news is that I don't know if Tom was able to request the records we need. All we have is the list of names."

"Won't the army assign another intelligence officer?"

"I went to Tom as a friend." He turned left on County Line Road. This area was more rural, and soon there was very little traffic around them. "But you make a good point. It may be time to go through official channels."

"I agree. Surely, they'll cooperate with providing us the information we need."

"No, they won't keep us informed of the investigation." It was the main reason he'd avoided going the official route. The army was good at a lot of things, but communication down to the rank and file generally was not one of them. Information was ruthlessly protected under the premise of need-to-know.

"That's not right." Shelby sounded upset. "Why wouldn't they tell us what's going on?"

Before he could answer, the disposable cell phone rang.

"Brady, is that you?" Shelby asked. "I'm putting you on speaker again."

"Okay, I have a place you can use," Brady said. "It's located in Ravenswood, though. That's a bit of a hike from your current location."

Aiden took note of the sign for Highway 164. "We can get to Ravenswood, no problem. Did the feds provide this place?"

"Marc Callahan took care of it; his name should provide enough anonymity," Brady said. "It's clean, has three small bedrooms, but nothing fancy." His brother rattled off the address. "Think you can find it?"

"Yes." There was a white car behind him that had followed him through the last two turns. Using a white car as a tail would be unusual, but he wasn't taking any chances. "We'll find it."

"Call me when you get there," Brady said. "I'll keep digging on my end."

"Okay. Thanks." He felt calmer now that they had a solid destination in mind. He waited until the last possible moment to speed up and veer off the road and onto the interstate on-ramp. He smiled grimly when the white car kept going. He pushed the Jeep SUV even faster, determined to cover as much distance as possible in case the driver of the white car turned around to continue following them.

"Is there someone behind us?" Shelby twisted in her seat.

"No." He didn't want her to worry. "We're clear."

She settled back. "Ravenswood is south of Milwaukee, near the lakeshore, right?"

"Yes. But I doubt the safe house will be anywhere near the lakefront." He managed a small smile. "Those places cost megabucks."

She didn't answer. When he glanced over his shoulder, he noticed she was staring out the window, her fingers twisted tightly in her lap.

His chest ached with how frightened she was. And while they'd managed to escape once again, he could tell this constantly being on the move made her anxious. Considering they had a three-year-old to take care of, too, he understood.

After the shooting attack on Tom Mitchell, he believed they were on the right track. That these attempts to kill Shelby must be related to her husband's infidelity.

Everything about this situation screamed personal attack.

He pushed the speed limit, moving from one lane to the next in an effort to ensure the white car didn't catch up. If the guy was even tailing him in the first place. In truth, his imagination could be working overtime.

There was no way for him to know where the next threat would come from. And that was the most frustrating thing of all.

Traffic during the early afternoon was light, and they made good time reaching Ravenswood. He didn't have a smart phone, but the dashboard of the Jeep had a GPS map, so he found the safe house location without any difficulty.

The house was small and white, situated in the center

of a small city lot. There were houses on either side, but no sign of people out and about. He pulled into the driveway, then turned in his seat. "Could I have my phone back?"

She nodded. "This place looks nice."

"It will do." At least for now. He called Brady who immediately answered. "We're here. Is there a code to get in?"

"Yes, there's a push button lock on the back door. The code is 4761."

"Got it." He paused, then added, "Are you heading over?"

"On my way. See you soon." His brother ended the call.

"Let's get inside." He didn't like leaving the SUV parked in the driveway and would arrange to use the detached garage once Brady was here. For now, the sooner they were situated inside the house, the better.

"No swimming?" Eva's lower lip trembled as Shelby unbuckled her car seat strap. "I wanna go back to the pool."

"Hey, we'll find something fun to do." What, he had no clue. He wanted to sweep the little girl into his arms but pulled their bags and computer case out from the back seat instead. "Let's get inside."

"No!" Eva was working herself into a tantrum. Aiden shot Shelby a helpless look. He hadn't dealt with this on the two occasions he'd taken Caleb to the zoo.

"Okay, you can sit out here alone." Shelby turned and walked away from the car. Aiden stared at her, it wasn't safe to leave the little girl behind, but he needn't have worried.

Eva nimbly crawled from the car seat. "Mommy, wait! I'm coming."

"I'm glad." Shelby turned and calmly waited for Eva to catch up.

Crisis averted, he closed the car door and locked the

vehicle. Then he went to the side door of the house. He punched in the key code and held it open for Shelby and Eva. One good thing about staying in a single-family home rather than a hotel room was that there were at least two doors leading out of the house. Not to mention the myriad of windows.

Hotel rooms made him nervous when they only had one way in or out. He and his siblings had been in more than one dicey situation where that lack of egress had posed a problem. Look what had almost happened at the American Lodge?

The place was neat and clean. Nothing fancy as Brady had mentioned. But nicer than the American Lodge motel. Peering through the windows, he noticed the houses on either side were fairly close. Winter weather meant keeping windows and doors closed anyway, so he hoped their proximity to the neighbors wouldn't be cause for concern.

Frankly, the way things were going, Aiden doubted they'd be in Ravenswood for long.

"Let's play with your dolly," Shelby said, distracting Eva with her toys.

Thankfully, the little girl cradled the baby doll in her arms, talking nonstop. While Eva and Shelby were busy, he took the time to unpack the computer. He lifted the cover of the laptop, knowing Brady would have made sure there was Wi-Fi access here. Another perk of staying in a single-family house was having a secure internet network.

Aiden booted up the computer and searched the house for a router. He found the password helpfully written along the top of the device. He was on the internet within seconds, then turned his attention to the names Tom Mitchell had provided.

Time to get to work. One of the female soldiers on this list had to be involved in the rumored affair.

And he would start with the three who had ultimately left the service in the last two years.

---

SHELBY COULDN'T SETTLE DOWN. While keeping Eva preoccupied, she moved from one window to the next, peering out anxiously, as if she would know a suspicious vehicle if she saw one.

Being fearful and on edge was foreign to her. Her life before this was boring. Relatively predictable. At least as far as her job and homelife were concerned. She and Eva had settled into a routine, with her father's help on occasion to fill in the gaps like when she had parent-teacher conferences.

Now? Her life was a twisty, gut-churning roller coaster. With more lows than highs. One she wanted to get off from.

But it seemed as if this head-snapping ride would go on and on, with no end in sight.

When Aiden's phone rang, she startled so badly she smacked her elbow on the window. Turning, she caught him eyeing her quizzically as he answered the phone.

"Hey, Brady. What's up?" There was a pause, then Aiden said, "Okay. We're here. And frozen pizza for dinner is perfect. Thanks for thinking of it." He lowered the phone back to the table. "My brother will be here soon."

The news was slightly reassuring. In some ways, she wished all his cop siblings could be there. Strength in numbers.

"Did you try the television?" Aiden asked. "I'm sure they have cable."

"No, but that reminds me. We can connect the tablet Elly let us borrow to the internet, too, right?"

"Yes." He smiled gently. "Whatever works to keep Eva happy."

She was touched by how much he seemed to care. Then she sternly reminded herself that Aiden Finnegan was a nice guy in general. He wasn't treating them any differently than he would any other woman and child in trouble.

After getting the tablet connected to the internet, she downloaded a cartoon video. "Here, Eva. Sit on the sofa with your dolly."

The little girl settled against the cushions, holding Dolly close. Parenting could be trying at times, but she wouldn't give up a single moment of her time with her daughter.

Tears pricked her eyes. She turned away, wrestling with her emotions. This wasn't the time to melt down. Now when they were safe in a city that was far away from where they'd faced danger.

Swiping at her face, she tried to pull herself together.

Aiden must have noticed because he was at her side in a heartbeat. He wrapped his strong arm around her shoulders and tugged her close. "Hey, it's okay. Don't be upset. We're safe."

"For how long?" The question popped out before she could stop it. She turned into his embrace, burying her face against his chest.

"For as long as I'm alive. I promise, my family will protect us."

She nodded, knowing he was right. Why she was falling apart now, she had no clue.

"Please, Shelby." His voice was a husky whisper in her ear. "It pains me to see you like this."

"I'm sorry." She squeezed her eyes shut to stop the tears.

"Don't apologize." He swept his hand down her hair to the center of her back. "I'm here for you, no matter what."

It was possibly the nicest thing a man had said to her in the two years since losing Emmitt.

After reveling in Aiden's warm embrace, she found the strength to pull herself together. Crying was useless. And really, they were safe. Their latest mad dash from the Timberland Falls Suites had been a preemptive move.

She should be relieved no gunfire had been involved.

"Thanks." She lifted her head and tried to ease out of his arms. "I guess I needed a hug."

"No need to thank me. We're in this together. And hey, I'm always ready to give out hugs." Aiden's smile warmed her heart. Then his gaze dropped to her mouth.

She knew he was about to kiss her. Shelby found herself moving closer, anticipating the kiss. Which was strange because she hadn't been interested in anyone since —forever.

His warm lips brushed hers, keeping the caress light. It wasn't nearly enough, but then she heard the sound of a car engine and realized why he'd pulled back so quickly.

Brady had arrived.

"He always did have rotten timing," Aiden muttered, releasing her. His disgruntled expression made her want to laugh.

How was it that she was able to find joy and happiness in a time like this?

Aiden flashed a rueful smile, then crossed to the side door. He opened it, allowing a wave of cold air to sneak inside. "Brady? I'd like the rental to be parked in the garage and out of sight."

"Give me the keys, I'll take care of it."

Aiden tossed the key fob through the door, then closed it. "Brr. I think the temperature dropped ten degrees in the past ten minutes."

She frowned and glanced toward the windows. Dark clouds were rolling in too. She inwardly groaned. The last thing they needed was a snowstorm.

Then again, maybe the change in weather would slow down the gunman stalking her. *If so*, she thought with a sigh, *bring on the snow*.

A few minutes later, Brady came into the house. To her surprise, he had an armful of toys. "I brought a few things for Eva."

The sweet and thoughtful gesture brought another prick of tears. "Thanks so much."

Eva perked up as Brady set the toy cars on the floor. She came over to sit down beside them, pushing them along the length of the carpet. Brady stepped back, watching with a smile. He glanced at her and shrugged. "My son is six, so we're long on cars and trucks."

"They're perfect. You know as well as I do kids love anything that's different from their own toys." She couldn't believe he'd taken the time to grab them.

Brady nodded, then turned to join Aiden at the kitchen table. After making sure Eva was okay, she followed. She wanted to know what, if anything, the Finnegans had uncovered.

"I backed into the garage." Brady dropped the key fob on the table. Aiden scooped it up and tucked it into his pocket. "Just in case you need to make a quick getaway."

"Thanks." Aiden pushed the list of names toward him. "We're operating under the theory that these attacks against Shelby are personal. Possibly related to an extramarital affair between Emmitt Copeland and another soldier."

Brady frowned, glancing at her. "You knew about it?"

"No." She wondered how many times she'd have to deny the allegation. "If I did, I'd have mentioned it after the first episode of gunfire."

Brady lifted his hands. "Okay, sorry. I had to ask."

Did he? She arched a brow. "Does it matter if I knew about it? Emmitt died two years ago. I'm still not clear on why anyone would seek revenge now."

"Mitchell thought Shelby's father, Sergeant Major Savage, may have discovered the truth recently and took action against the female soldier involved," Aiden said. "That would explain the recent attacks."

"Maybe." Brady frowned. "But what's the worst that could happen? A dishonorable discharge? Pretty lame to shoot someone over that."

"Not necessarily," Aiden said. "A dishonorable discharge makes it difficult to get work in the civilian world."

"Okay, but a soldier having an affair can't be the worst thing in the world. I mean, there are far worse crimes, right? Assault, battery, et cetera. Big jump from a dishonorable discharge to murder," Brady protested.

"Maybe something else happened." Shelby glanced at the two men. It wasn't easy to discuss her husband's affair. "You mentioned assault and battery. Wouldn't that be a reason to seek revenge?"

"Honestly, I'm having trouble understanding why anyone would target a woman and child." Aiden let out a frustrated sigh. "No matter what the allegation, or the action taken by your father, murdering innocents is not typical payback from a soldier's perspective."

"Yeah, that's been troubling me too," Brady agreed.

"That brings us back to this being a personal attack on Shelby."

A horrible thought hit hard. "What if the female soldier didn't know Emmitt was married?"

Aiden's brown eyes widened. "He didn't wear a wedding ring?"

"No." She remembered how they'd argued about that. "Emmitt insisted that he couldn't wear one while on deployments."

"What about your father? Did he wear one?"

"My mother died when I was in college." She thought back. "I believe he did wear one, but he held a higher rank than Emmitt, so I didn't think much about it."

"We are allowed to wear a plain wedding band," Aiden said softly. "No stones or anything like that, even for the women. But there is no such thing as not being allowed to wear a simple wedding band."

She tried not to wince. "I see. Well, that proves my point. Emmitt didn't wear a wedding ring, and it's possible the woman he was sleeping with didn't know he had a wife and daughter."

"Okay, but wouldn't she have attended Emmitt's funeral?" Aiden asked. "You and Eva were there, Shelby. No secret that you were his wife and Eva his daughter. Especially with your father standing beside you while you were offered the flag. And that was two years ago, which doesn't explain these recent attacks."

He was right, nothing made sense. "I don't know. Maybe she missed the funeral."

Brady was scrolling through his phone when Aiden said, "Are you listening? Do you have a theory?"

"Ah, sorry." Brady glanced up, his expression somber. "I asked my boss, Donovan, if he could reach out to the Army

Intelligence Office. I mentioned how Lieutenant Tom Mitchell may have been followed and attacked after meeting with you." He held up his phone. "Donovan just texted me back. 'I'm sorry to tell you both that Tom Mitchell died at the scene, and there was no sign of the shooter when the police arrived.'"

Dead. The one man who'd agreed to help them figure out what was going on was dead! She met Aiden's stricken gaze, silently praying they wouldn't be next.

# CHAPTER SEVEN

The news of Tom's death was like a sucker punch to the gut. Aiden sat in stunned silence for a long moment. "This perp is escalating. Apparently, he'll eliminate anyone who gets in his way."

"Yeah, it's not good," Brady agreed. His brother's concerned gaze landed on Shelby, then over at Eva. "I'm glad you got out of that hotel when you did."

"This time." He scrubbed a hand over his face. "The shooter seemed to know about Tom's intent to investigate the shooting. Why wait so long after Tom left the hotel to kill him? That time gap is strange, unless Tom didn't hit the road right away."

"Maybe he stopped for lunch," Brady suggested.

That was entirely possible. "Okay, maybe. But as far as I know, Tom hadn't told anyone except his boss that he was coming to meet with us. Makes me wonder if the shooter is still active army."

"Or has connections to active army intelligence," Brady said.

"What are we going to do now?" Shelby asked in an anguished tone. "Who can we trust?"

It was a good question. He grimaced and shook his head, glancing at Brady. "I don't know. Do you have any ideas?"

Brady sighed. "I wish I did." He looked at Shelby. "Can you remember anyone in particular that your father worked with?"

Shelby looked as if she might cry, but then she abruptly straightened. "Wait. I received a phone call after my father's death from a Kevin Carter." She frowned, then added, "I had the impression he worked under my father. Maybe at the level of a first sergeant?"

Aiden leaned forward, nodding slowly. "I report to Kevin Carter. What did he want to talk to you about?"

Her brow furrowed. "He wanted to express his condolences, but then he asked if my father had brought home any files the day he died. I told him my father kept his military life separate from his personal life." She spread her hands. "My dad rarely brought work home with him."

The brief flare of anticipation fizzled out. "He wasn't more specific?"

"No." She looked upset. "I should have mentioned this sooner, but I didn't think much about it. I figured he was just looking for a specific file, nothing more." Her gaze swung from him to Brady and back again. "Do you think he's involved in this?"

"We shouldn't jump to conclusions," Aiden said thoughtfully. "But it does make me wonder if that file had details about your husband's death."

"The file could be anything," Brady said. "If the army is anything like the federal government, they love paperwork."

"I know, but one man is dead, and there have been several attempts to shoot Shelby." He hated feeling as if they were stumbling around in the dark. "I need to reach out to Carter."

"Hold on, bro." Brady scowled. "If he is involved, we can't risk allowing him to get our location."

"Let's start with the list of female soldiers, then." He tapped the sheet of paper. "Maybe we can see if any of these women are related to Carter. Or any other army officer."

"We can try, but there's no guarantee the relation has the same name. Could be a divorce, half sibling, et cetera," Shelby cautioned.

"I know." Aiden frowned and shrugged. "But we have to start somewhere."

"You get started on that. I need to call Donovan. He was going to reach out to the Army Intelligence Office but was sidetracked by the news of Tom Mitchell's death." Brady stood and moved out of the small kitchen area.

Pulling the computer close, he glanced over to the three women Mitchell had identified as recently leaving the army. He started with the first name, Kelly Darnell, typing it into social media. Shelby leaned close, her sweet scent teasing his senses as she watched him work.

It didn't take long to find the female soldier. Her social media profile listed her as formerly a member of the Army National Guard. From there, it was also easy to verify she was currently living in Alabama with her husband. She'd posted a picture of her husband and young daughter beneath a large sign that said, "Welcome Home." It appeared she'd gotten out of the army to spend more time with her family.

"They look so happy," Shelby murmured.

He glanced at her, disconcerted as to how close she was.

"I understand none of this is easy for you. But try to remember the good times rather than dwelling on the bad."

She averted her gaze. "I have a feeling the good times I remember aren't real." There was a trace of bitterness in her tone. "They were nothing more than a show Emmitt put on for us."

He couldn't come up with a good way to respond to that. "Let's put a check mark next to her name and move on. She doesn't come across as a viable suspect."

"Maybe she was leading a double life the way Emmitt was," Shelby protested.

Anything was possible, but they had to draw a line somewhere. "Let's try the next name."

It took a little longer this time to track down the female soldier, a woman by the name of Adrienne Cook. He found the one Adrienne Cook he believed to be the name on the list, but her profile was private. He stared at the woman's photo, trying to figure out how to find out more about her.

"It's killing me to know one of these women slept with Emmitt."

He eased his arm around her shoulders and hugged her. "His failures are not yours. Some guys just need the thrill of sneaking around."

"Maybe. But it's hard not to take this as a personal slap in the face. As if I wasn't good enough for him."

"Please don't think that." He hated hearing the self-doubt in her voice. "You and Eva are beautiful. If Emmitt wasn't satisfied with his perfect family, there was something seriously wrong with him. Not you."

"You're so sweet." She leaned against him for a moment, then straightened. "What if you searched on Emmitt Copeland and Adrienne Cook together?"

He did so, but the search yielded no results. Then he

tried Adrienne Cook along with the words Army National Guard.

This time, a picture did bloom on the screen. As a staff sergeant, he only had a dozen soldiers beneath him. None of these names were familiar to him, so it was no surprise to see that Adrienne Cook's small platoon was under another staff sergeant, Wade Norris. In the photo, Adrienne's expression was grim. She did not look happy to be there.

"We'll have to consider her a possible suspect." He tried not to sigh. "Let's move on to the last female who was recently discharged."

Justine Brooks was stunningly beautiful, classic features framed by honey-blond hair. Her eyes were a striking green, but so much so that he felt certain she wore tinted contact lenses. There was no doubt in his mind that Justine would have attracted a lot of male attention. As he eyed her photo, he vaguely recalled seeing her during one of their recent deployments. He wished he had access to her personnel record because he wanted to know what date she'd left the army. It must have been relatively recent.

"Do you know her?" Shelby asked.

"She was involved in a recent deployment, maybe three to four months ago." He remembered now. They'd been deployed to stand guard during a riot in Tennessee back in June. "She seemed like a decent soldier, held her ground well enough in a tough situation. But I know a lot of the guys wanted to date her."

"She's totally Emmitt's type," Shelby said, fingering her own blond hair.

He personally preferred Shelby's girl-next-door looks, but he didn't voice his opinion. "Okay, we'll consider her a suspect." The fact that she'd recently left the army nagged at him. Had Shelby's father discovered her affair with

Emmitt and forced the issue of her resignation? Even if he had, it was not easy to imagine this woman lying in wait at the funeral, shooting at Shelby and Eva.

Women could be every bit as lethal as men, but he still wasn't convinced this woman would seek revenge in the form of shooting and killing an innocent woman and child.

Brady returned to the kitchen. "Donovan has the name of another army intelligence officer, guy by the name of Heath Strauss."

Aiden frowned. "I never heard of him."

"Donovan told me Strauss has been assigned to investigate Tom Mitchell's death." Brady held his gaze. "And that means he wants to talk to you and Shelby."

No surprise there. "Only if we can meet at a neutral location. And only if you and some of the other sibs come to back us up."

Brady grinned. "I thought you'd say that, so I left a message with Reed, Tarin, Kyleigh, and Sami."

"I'm not sure we'll need all of them," he protested.

"Hey, they live for this stuff." Brady's smile faded. "Seriously, we'll make sure to have your back. And of course, Shelby's and Eva's too."

"They're the most important," Aiden said with a nod. "It would be nice if either Kyleigh or Sami would stand guard with them."

"Why, because they're women?" Brady shook his head. "Better not let Kyleigh or Sami hear you say that."

"I only mentioned the two women because Eva might be more comfortable with a female protector."

As if to prove him wrong, Eva came running over with a truck. She placed it in his lap, then gazed up at him. "Play wif me?"

Brady let out a snort of laughter. "Yeah, sure."

"Maybe later, Eva." He would have enjoyed nothing more than to play with the little girl, but he still had a list of names to review.

Too many names.

"I'll play with you." Shelby took the truck, then led her daughter back to the living room. He watched them for a minute, a flash of anger hitting hard at what Emmitt had done to her.

"Keep your head in the game," Brady warned. "Getting emotionally involved will cloud your judgment."

"Yeah, like you and all the rest of my older siblings haven't done that," he shot back. Then he sighed. "I know, you're right. What's the timeline on the meeting with Heath Strauss?"

"We may need to wait until tomorrow." Brady gestured to the window. "It's snowing like crazy out there. Setting up a neutral location and giving others enough time to come in to provide backup will likely take longer in the snowstorm."

"Tomorrow, then." He sighed. "In the meantime, I'll keep working on the list. Maybe I'll come up with something that will help point us in the right direction." He wanted to believe that, but in reality, he had a bad feeling they'd be lucky to eliminate even half the names from the list.

To be fair, he couldn't say with any certainty that their perp was on the list at all.

---

SHELBY SAT on the floor playing with Eva while listening to the conversation between Brady and Aiden.

"Hang on, this is Kyleigh now." Brady took a few steps away to chat with their sister.

She noticed Aiden returned to the top of the list, as if intending to complete a search on each woman in order. Envisioning the list, she remembered they were listed alphabetically by last name.

The image of Justine's stunning face was burned into her mind. She wanted to believe Emmitt hadn't cheated at all, but if he'd been tempted by a woman like Justine? Easy to see how he would have tripped over his own feet to get to her.

Aiden's words helped dull the sharp pain. Emmitt's failures weren't her fault. If he didn't want to be married anymore, then he should have asked for a divorce. She would have been shocked and upset by that, but learning of his infidelity was just as bad.

Maybe worse.

"Thanks, Kyleigh. I'll keep you updated on the timeline." Brady returned to the table to join Aiden. "Kyleigh is off tomorrow, so she's in. Tarin texted back that he's available too. Not bad for starters."

Aiden glanced at her, then nodded. "I figured the family would rally. Have you heard from Rhy about Devon?"

"Not yet." Brady's thumbs tapped on his phone screen. "Could be Devon is in labor right now, and if so, he probably won't let us know what's going on until he has news to share."

Their comment about Rhy and Devon being at the hospital about to give birth to their first child reminded her of how she'd delivered Eva all alone. Without Emmitt's support. The nursing staff and her OB physician had been wonderful, but she had been hyperaware of Emmitt's absence.

Looking back, the way he'd rushed in after Eva had

been born, looking embarrassed and ashamed, she couldn't help but wonder if he'd been with another woman during the time she'd sweated, groaned, cried, and pushed their daughter into the world.

Enough. She brought herself up short. There was no point in rehashing the lowest points of their relationship. As Aiden mentioned, there had been good times too. Besides, Emmitt was gone. Getting angry with him now was the epitome of useless.

"Looks like Reed can be here tomorrow too," Brady said, interrupting her thoughts. "But Sami is out. She's working."

"Three extra guns are more than enough," Aiden said. "You and I will be armed too. That's plenty. Can you find a place to have this meeting? Someplace where we can make sure to have the area secured first?"

"I'll find another house to rent." Brady looked up from his phone screen. "Someplace like this would be easy enough to defend. But I also need to hit the road to pick up Grace and Caleb."

"Sounds good, but be careful out there." Aiden glanced up from his computer with a frown. "You should have left earlier."

"It's okay." Brady walked to the door. "I'll be in touch with the rest of the plan soon."

Aiden nodded, then turned back to the computer. He appeared to be attacking the list with a vengeance.

After another thirty minutes passed, Eva thrust her toys away as if bored with them. "Mommy, I'm hungry,"

"Okay." She rose to her feet. The snow was coming down hard now, making it difficult to see the traffic passing by on the street. She was surprised to realize it was five thirty in the evening. "I'll throw the frozen pizza in now, if that's okay with you."

"Perfect." Aiden glanced over. "Thanks."

It took her a moment to figure out how to work the oven. While it preheated, she unwrapped the plain cheese pizza. Chosen by Brady, she was sure, for Eva's sake.

Eva began to get antsy, enough that Aiden was forced to push the computer away. "Okay, Eva, we need to set the table."

She was touched by how Aiden helped Eva with the simple task. He was so sweet and attentive she had to glance away.

This—being together like this was temporary. Aiden was a great guy, but if she ever decided to get romantically involved—and that was a big if—it would not be with another soldier.

No way, no how.

When the pizza was finished, she removed it from the oven and cut it into squares. Eva seemed to think all pizza should be cut into squares because that was how pizza delivery service worked.

Aiden grinned when he saw it. "Tastes better that way, doesn't it?"

She smiled. "If you say so."

"Hungry, hungry." Eva bounced from one foot to the other.

"Bathroom first." She took her daughter's hand and steered her to the half bath. When they finished, she found Aiden waiting patiently for them.

"I'd like to say grace." Once they were seated, Eva on a pillow, Aiden reached for her hand. "Dear Lord Jesus, we thank You for this food we are about to eat. We also thank You for keeping us safe in Your care. Please continue to guide us to safety. Amen."

"Amen." She gently squeezed his hand, then reached

for Eva's plate. She took a tiny bite herself first to make sure it wasn't too hot. Then proceeded to set two small pieces on the plate.

"Have you found anything?" She eyed Aiden as they dug into the meal. She was used to cheese pizza but suspected he would have preferred one with the works.

"Not yet." He frowned. "It's taking longer than I like. So far, Justine seems the most likely candidate. When we meet with Heath Strauss, I'm hoping to learn more about the circumstances of when and why she left the army."

She nodded, hoping this new army investigator would be a help rather than a hindrance. Horrifying to realize Tom Mitchell was dead just because he'd tried to help them.

Especially her.

Trusting a new guy would not be easy. Listening while Brady had arranged for Finnegan backup for the meeting was humbling. At first, she'd wondered if the Finnegans were too good to be true. Hard to imagine that such a large family could be so close. But now she knew they were for real. Dropping everything to respond to Aiden's request at the drop of a hat.

"More," Eva announced.

"More, please," she corrected.

"Pease," Eva obediently repeated.

She took another square from the pizza and set it on Eva's plate, then glanced at Aiden. "Is there something I can do to help? I feel so useless."

His warm smile made her heart kick into high gear. "You're helping by making dinner and playing with Eva."

"I want Mr. Aiden to play wif me," Eva said around a mouth full of pizza.

"Maybe later, if you're good," Aiden said. "But you have to listen to your mom."

"I always listen to Mommy." The little girl's gaze was earnest, as if she'd never misbehaved a day in her life.

Hilarious.

"When we're finished eating, I'd like to have you review some of these photos." Aiden turned to her. "I'd like to know if these women look familiar."

"I highly doubt Emmitt would have brought one of them home for introductions."

"No, I was thinking more about if one might look familiar from attending his funeral."

She stared at her plate for a long moment. "I don't remember much about that day. I know that sounds horrible, but I was still in shock. My dad handled all the details." At the time she was grateful for the help, but when her dad had died, she'd had to figure out everything on her own. It may have been better for her to have been more involved in Emmitt's funeral.

"It's okay. If you don't recognize anyone, that's fine." He reached over to clasp her hand in his. "I'd just like you to try."

"Of course." She'd offered to help after all. And she needed to do her part in trying to figure out who was trying to kill her. That anyone could hate her and Eva that much was still difficult to comprehend. "Maybe something will come to me."

"That's my hope," Aiden agreed.

When they'd finished eating, she cleared the table, wiped liberal smears of tomato sauce off Eva's face and hands, then set up her daughter with the tablet again. So much for cutting down on screen time. She crossed to the sink to begin washing dishes. When Aiden came over to help, she waved him off. "I'm fine. I'd rather you keep working the list."

"Thanks." He returned to the kitchen table and opened the laptop.

The lights flickered but stayed on. She froze, then glanced at Aiden who shrugged. "Not much I can do if the power goes out."

Maybe not, but the furnace going out could be a problem. She tried to think positively. Even a gunman would think twice about trying to find her in a snowstorm. And maybe he or she would end up driving off the road or getting stuck in a ditch.

Leaving the dishes to air dry, she joined Aiden at the table, steeling herself to see more gorgeous women who may or may not have had an affair with her deceased husband.

"I saved their profile pictures on the screen." Aiden opened the first one. She stared at it, then shook her head.

"No, I'm sorry."

"Don't apologize. I'm just asking." He minimized that photo, then pulled up another. When she shook her head, he moved onto the third. Then a fourth. All were pretty enough, but none as stunning as Justine. "This is the last one. I didn't get as far as I'd hoped."

There was something familiar about the fifth woman. She frowned, trying to place her. "This one may have been at Emmitt's funeral. I'm sorry, but I just can't say so for sure."

"Okay, this is Donna Olson." He paused, then added, "I'll add her to the possible suspect list."

She sighed and nodded. "I wish I was more help."

"We are both doing our best here," he said in a low voice. "Let's take credit for that."

"I'm not normally a negative Nelly," she said on a sigh. "I am grateful for everything you're doing for me. For us."

She glanced back at Eva. "The way your family has rallied around you is amazing."

"Oh, we all like to get up inside each other's business," he said in a teasing tone. When his phone rang, he grinned. "Speaking of the family, this is Rhy." He lifted the phone to his ear. "Hey, Rhy. How's Devon?"

He didn't put the call on speaker, so she couldn't hear his brother's side of the conversation.

"Congrats on your new daughter! What's her name? Aw, really? Colleen? Naming her after our mother is a wonderful idea. I'm sure Mom is grinning down from heaven."

"Tell him congrats from me," she whispered.

"Shelby wants you to know she's happy for you, too, Rhy. Yes, we're safe. Focus on your new family. Brady, Tarin, and Reed are helping us out. Later." He lowered the phone. "I had a feeling Devon was having a girl. Rhy thought so, too. But Devon insisted the baby was a boy."

"Usually it's the men who want boys," she said.

"Neither of them cares one way or the other. They'll both love any child God gives them. But it's no secret that boys are predominant in both the Finnegan and Callahan families." He smiled. "Six boys and only three girls."

"Then I'm glad Colleen has been born to balance things out."

The lights flickered again, making her wince. "I should probably get Eva ready for bed soon. Once the lights go out, she won't have the tablet or TV to keep her occupied."

He nodded. "I just want to check this next name, Amy Golden. Then we can call it a night." He typed the name into the social media search engine, and the first thing that came up was an obituary.

"She died?" A chill snaked down her spine upon seeing

the young woman's smiling face in the center of the death announcement.

"Yeah. I wasn't expecting that." He typed a few more keys, then sat back in his chair, looking dazed. "Amy Golden committed suicide three weeks ago."

Suicide. The word hung dark and heavy between them. The timeline of being three weeks ago was eerie too. Was it possible this young woman's death was related to what was happening now?

# CHAPTER EIGHT

Ten minutes after he'd stumbled across Amy Golden's obituary, the power went out. Aiden had found a small flashlight in the junk drawer after the first time the lights had flickered, so he gladly reached for it now. In the dim light, he caught Shelby's stricken gaze.

They were both shaken over the discovery that one of the women on the list had died of suicide.

"May I use the flashlight for a bit?" Shelby asked.

"Of course." He handed it over.

"Thanks. Come with me, Eva. Time to get ready for bed." Shelby took her daughter into the bathroom.

He sat at the kitchen table in the darkness, his thoughts whirling. Suicides among those in law enforcement and the military were not unheard of. Easy access to a weapon and the devastation they witnessed while being on the job could push people to the brink. Having faith and trust in God's plan wasn't always enough.

He understood some people struggled with depression. Had that been true with Amy Golden's case? He wasn't sure what to think about regarding the timing of her death. Was her suicide related to the shooting spree going on now? She'd been a pretty girl, not as stunning as Justine Brooks, but he supposed it was possible she'd been seeing Emmitt. But even if she had been having an affair with Shelby's husband, why would she take her life now? Two years after his death?

The darkness was offset by the white snow piling up outside. Through the windows, he noticed the reflection of the streetlights off the snow was enough to illuminate the living room and kitchen.

He heard Shelby murmuring to Eva as she tucked the little girl into bed. Rising to his feet, he moved from window to window, searching for anything unusual.

It appeared as if the blanket of snow had put the neighborhood to sleep. There wasn't even so much as a car driving down the road.

"Good night, Aiden." Shelby's low voice had him turning from the window. She held out the flashlight. "I'm going to sleep with Eva, she's scared."

"Sounds good. Get some rest." He wanted to kiss her but remained where he was, unwilling to make her feel uncomfortable by crossing the line. Bad enough they were stuck in the safe house, living as if they were a family. Oddly enough, he found he liked it. "Good night."

She smiled and turned away. He waited until the bedroom door was closed behind her before letting out his pent-up breath. He needed to keep his mind on the mission. On the task of keeping Shelby and her daughter safe from harm.

Nothing more.

He made one more sweep of the house, going into each

of the rooms except for where Shelby and Eva were sleeping, before stretching out to get some shut-eye for himself. It wasn't likely the gunman would find them at the house Brady had secured for them.

The faces of the female soldiers he'd checked out flashed in his mind, one after another as if they were a slideshow. The key to identifying the shooter had to be within this list. He finally managed to shut down his brain long enough to pray for strength and guidance, and then he fell asleep.

A muted sound woke him. He blinked in the darkness, then shifted up onto his elbow. Peering at his watch, he noticed it was four in the morning. He rolled out of bed and grabbed his pistol. Then he eased out of the room to make his way through to the main living area.

There was no sign of Shelby or Eva, but he thought they must have woken him up. The kitchen and living room lights were still off, and there was a distinct chill in the air, indicating the power had not been restored.

He frowned, scanning the five inches of snow covering the ground outside. Easy to see why they'd lost power, but if it didn't come back on soon, they'd have to leave to find a motel. It would be too cold in here for a three-year-old.

He made a mental note that when he was ready to buy a place of his own, he'd make sure there was either a fireplace or a woodburning stove for times like this. Winter in Wisconsin was no joke.

A hint of movement outside caught his eye. Easing closer to the window that faced the road, he scanned the area. The snow appeared undisturbed for as far as he could see. The city plows hadn't even been through yet, although he suspected they would be out soon. Even though it was a weekend, people still needed to get to work. Especially first responders.

There were deep ruts in the road from where some cars had driven past. But there was a thin layer of snow covering them, so he didn't think anyone had been out there in at least an hour or so.

Thankfully, the snow had stopped. He was about to turn away from the window when he saw the shadow again.

He froze. His gaze zoomed in on a dark shadow moving near the house to the left. It was located on the opposite side from where the driveway and garage for their rental property was located.

The shadow moved again, creeping ever so slowly from the front of the house next door toward the backyard. Who was out there? He couldn't imagine how anyone could have found their current location, but he also wasn't about to take any chances.

He shoved the computer into the bag and slung it over his shoulder. Then he stuffed as many of the small trucks and cars Brady had brought inside too. He picked up Shelby's and Eva's coats, then slipped into their bedroom.

"What is it?" Shelby asked in a whisper. He wasn't sure if he'd woken her by coming in or if she'd already been awake.

"We need to go. Put your coat on first, then wake Eva to put hers on. We'll leave through the back door. You'll have to carry her to the garage."

Without warning the power flashed on. He froze, feeling like a deer caught in headlights, then lunged for the switch, killing the lights.

Shelby had already tugged on her coat and shoes, then had reached for her daughter. Rather than wrestling the sleeping toddler into her winter coat, Shelby wrapped her in a blanket and lifted her from the bed.

"Ready." Her voice was calm, but her wide, anxious eyes shone with fear.

He would have offered to carry Eva, but he needed to be able to shoot if necessary. They moved silently through the house to the back door. Stepping to the side, he leaned close. "Walk quickly to the garage and punch in the code 4-7-1 to unlock the side door. I'll be right behind you."

She gave a curt nod, then opened the door. He didn't like sending her out first, but there wasn't a better option. The snow muffled the sound of them moving across the small yard, but the deep footprints they'd leave behind were like neon signs announcing the path they'd taken.

He held his weapon with both hands, sweeping them from side to side as he hurried after Shelby. There was no sign of the intruder.

The small keypad on the garage door lit up after Shelby entered the code. He stepped up to the opening, then stood with his back to the garage. He'd stand guard until Shelby and Eva were safe inside the SUV.

A dark figure rushed out from between the two houses. Even though he was prepared, the move surprised him. Aiden fired his weapon, mostly to scare the guy off, before ducking into the garage and slamming the door behind him.

Sending up a prayer of thanks for Brady's ingenious decision to back into the garage, he slid in behind the wheel. He hit the button to open the garage door. Upon hearing the sound of gunfire, he realized there was no time to waste.

He sent up a silent prayer of thanks that the power had returned in time to open the garage door. Yet it seemed to move with incredible slowness. Shifting into four-wheel drive, he punched the gas and sent the Jeep SUV lunging forward. The thin aluminum garage door crumpled like a cookie as the vehicle rolled through.

"What in the world?"

"Keep your head down!" There was no time for reassurances. At least Shelby and Eva were in the back seat. All four tires on the Jeep managed to get good traction through the deep snow. Yet they weren't going fast enough to satisfy him.

Especially not when more gunfire rang out.

He barreled out of the driveway and fishtailed a bit when he turned left. The ruts in the road enabled him to pick up speed. Glancing back in the rearview mirror, he caught a glimpse of the dark figure running in the opposite direction.

Did the intruder have a car nearby? The thought made him press on, taking several turns to get far away from the rental property.

"How did—h-he find us?" Shelby's teeth were chattering, so he twisted the heat to full blast.

"I have no idea." He didn't like this turn of events one bit. "Are you okay back there?"

"Y-yes." He suspected Shelby was far from okay, but she and Eva weren't physically hurt, which is what really mattered. "I—need to get Eva in her car seat."

"Soon." He didn't want to slow down or pull over yet. At this hour of the morning, traffic was nonexistent. It wouldn't take long for the intruder to catch up with them, especially if he had a four-wheel-drive vehicle too.

He took the shortest distance to the interstate, relieved to see that the major thoroughfare had been plowed. Keeping a wary eye on the rearview mirror, he watched for signs of being followed. There was no one behind them.

So far, so good.

Pushing his speed as much as he dared, Aiden left the city of Ravenswood. When reaching Greenland, he exited the freeway, then pulled over to the side of the road.

"Mommy, I hav'ta go to the bafroom." Eva rubbed her eyes.

"I know, sweetie." Shelby met his gaze in the rearview.

"I hear you. We'll find a place." Most gas stations opened early, but that may not be the case on a Saturday after a snowstorm. Once Eva was in her car seat with her coat on, he searched for the closest one.

They pulled up just as the dayshift clerk flipped the lights on. He drove around to the farthest corner of the building, away from the main road to avoid being seen. It was hardly foolproof since there was no way to hide two adults and a young child.

"I'll carry her," he offered. Shelby gratefully stepped back so he could gather the little girl into his arms.

They hurried inside. He sent the clerk an apologetic glance, saying, "We'll buy something for breakfast while we're here," as he strode directly to the restrooms.

Shelby took over from there, ushering Eva inside.

As before, he stood guard, waiting for them to finish. The enticing scent of coffee helped him relax.

They'd gotten away from the intruder. There were too many possible directions for them to have gone, so he believed they were safe. At least for the moment.

But for how long? That was the troubling question.

When Shelby and Eva emerged from the restrooms, he headed over to the coffee machine. "Can you find something here for Eva to eat for breakfast?"

"Yes. We should eat something too." Shelby's expression was weary. He wished he could reassure her they'd be safe. But every time he'd thought he'd accomplished that mission, he was proven wrong.

"Grab whatever you need." He chose a bacon-and-egg sandwich that he had to nuke in the microwave and a cup of coffee. Carrying both the sandwich and the coffee to the counter, he walked back to help Shelby with her items.

After he'd paid for their breakfast meals, coffee, and chocolate milk for Eva, they headed back outside. The area appeared deserted, but he didn't intend to linger.

Minutes later, he was relieved to be back on the road. Yet he couldn't completely relax his guard. Not until he was absolutely sure there was no one following them.

Then again, they hadn't been followed to the rental property either. Look how that had turned out? They'd been found. But not right away. It had taken almost fifteen hours for the intruder to arrive on scene.

There were only two possibilities as to how this perp had found them. The house had been rented under Marc Callahan's name. Maybe his brother's boss, special agent in charge of the Milwaukee FBI office, had spoken to someone in the army about Brady's involvement and that person dug deep enough to find the house rented in Marc's name. Maybe they assumed the two federal agents knew each other. Or they'd somehow stumbled across the family connection. The Finnegans and Callahans being related wasn't a secret. Anyone with access to a DNA site would see it.

Or the new Army Intelligence Officer Heath Strauss had found the link. He may, in fact, have been the guy outside the property.

Neither option was remotely reassuring.

SHE AND EVA would never be safe again.

Shelby struggled not to break down into uncontrollable sobs. It felt as if this nightmare would never end.

It wasn't Aiden's fault. He was doing his best. Hadn't he gotten them out of there in the nick of time? Yet somehow, even with the amazingly supportive manpower of the Finnegan family, they couldn't escape the shooter.

Maybe they never would.

The depressing thought threatened to overwhelm her, but then Aiden said, "We need to pray, to thank God for this blessing."

"What blessing?" The words shot out of her mouth before she could stop them.

"I know this has been difficult, but we are safe." He met her gaze in the rearview mirror. "God is watching over us."

"He needs to do more." She hated sounding like an ungrateful child. But hadn't they been through enough already?

How much more did God expect them to take?

"Don't lose faith." Aiden's voice was soft. "Please, Shelby. Don't lose faith."

She swallowed hard and looked away.

"Dear Lord, we ask You to bless this food and to continue keeping us safe in Your care. Amen."

Despite her anger at God, she found herself bowing her head and silently echoing his amen. She still wasn't satisfied, but there wasn't anything she could do about that now.

She wasn't hungry but made sure Eva ate her breakfast. The little girl was thrilled with the chocolate milk treat. When the little girl was full, she forced herself to take a few small bites of her now cold sandwich.

Aiden ate his breakfast sandwich in four bites, then pulled out his cell phone. "Brady, call me back when you get this message." Aiden lowered the disposable phone into the cupholder in the center console.

"I'm not sure we can trust the FBI." She tucked a strand of her hair behind her ear. She'd finger combed it in the gas station bathroom but didn't get all the tangles out. "Or this new army investigator."

He surprised her by nodding in agreement. "I share your concerns. But we need to talk to someone within the army."

She hated to admit he was right. Whatever was going on here had roots in the armed forces.

"Don't forget, my family will back us up." Aiden smiled reassuringly. "We'll be okay."

Would they be okay? She wished she could be so sure.

Aiden's phone rang, and she was glad he put the call on speaker. "We're on the road and need a place to stay."

"You were found at the rental?" Brady's tone was incredulous. "How?"

"You tell me." Aiden slowed to a stop at the intersection. "Had to have been either Donovan or the new guy, Strauss."

"My boss is clean," Brady said quickly. "We've been able to trust him in the past."

"Donovan spoke to someone within the army. We need to know who that was," Aiden said. "I'm getting a bad feeling that the shooter is related to someone with a lot of brass."

"Yeah." Brady's tone sounded thoughtful. "I'll talk to Donovan."

"We still need to set up the meeting with Heath Strauss." Aiden met her gaze in the rearview. "He could be the leak, too, although that's less likely."

"Why?" She wasn't following his logic. "Maybe this was

his plan all along. To eliminate Tom Mitchell just so he could take over the investigation."

"Anything is possible," Brady said.

"True, but I'm still leaning toward this being a part of Emmitt's infidelity." She listened as Aiden explained about the female soldier named Amy Golden and how she'd committed suicide. "One theory is that Amy killed herself because she was unable to live with the guilt of having an affair with a married man. Now her father, brother, whoever is closest to her is out for revenge. Since the guy seeking revenge on her behalf can't target Copeland himself, Shelby and her daughter are the next best option."

"Suicide is an interesting angle." Brady paused, then added, "First you need a place to stay. Let me check with Tarin about the safe house. He mentioned it might be available soon."

"The one with bulletproof windows?" Aiden asked. "That would be nice."

"Yeah, it was being used, but it can't hurt to ask. Keep moving, I'll be in touch." The call went silent.

She thought about Aiden's theory. "We need to find out if Amy Golden has family, brothers, sisters, or parents."

"Yeah. I was going to do that, then the power went out." He turned at the next intersection and headed in a different direction. She hoped they didn't end up burning an entire tank of gas while waiting to get to another safe house.

She had to agree, one with bullet-resistant windows sounded ideal.

The snowplows were out in full force, which slowed their progress a bit. Not that they had a firm destination. In her mind, driving around wasn't much safer than sitting in a single-family home.

A full twenty minutes passed before Brady called back. "Okay, Tarin has the safe house ready. Here's the address."

Aiden typed the address into the GPS screen on the SUV. "Got it. We're about fifteen miles away. Could take longer to get there in the snow."

"Be safe, there's no rush. I have the rest of the crew meeting us there too." Brady said something in the background. "No, Caleb, you can't play with Eva today. Maybe another time." Then he spoke into the phone. "Sorry about that, the day care is obviously closed today, so Grace and Caleb are here with me. Anyway, we'll all meet at the safe house in an hour or less, okay?"

"Is there a code to get in?" Aiden asked.

"Yes. Hang on." There were rustling sounds, then Brady said, "Tarin used the last four digits of Rhy's cell phone."

"Got it. Thanks, Brady. We'll see you soon."

"Yes, oh, and just so you know, I have Marc Callahan joining us too."

"Wait a minute," Shelby protested. "Who is that? I don't think we should add anyone who isn't a Finnegan or related to one."

"The Callahans are related to the Finnegans," Brady said with a chuckle. "And most if not all of the Callahans have helped us out over the past year. We can trust them, Shelby. I promise."

Aiden nodded. "He's right. They're second cousins or something like that. We share the same set of great-grandparents. And Marc is also with the FBI. The more federal resources at our disposal, the better."

"Okay." She sat back in her seat. "More is better."

"Maybe not always, but absolutely in situations like this when you need backup," Brady said. "See you soon."

"Bye." Aiden ended the call, then hit the brake as a sedan fishtailed in the road ahead of them. The driver managed to stay on the road. "And that's why I like having four-wheel drive."

She couldn't argue with that assessment. Even though the schools often closed during storms, they didn't always get enough notice. She'd driven through plenty of storms. "You haven't seen anyone following us?"

"No. Very few people are out today, which is good. It's a weekend, so most are smart enough to stay home unless they absolutely need to get to work."

*Or if they're on the run from a vicious gunman.*

She sighed and turned her attention to Eva who was getting antsy. Her daughter did not love long car rides. And now that she was fully awake, Eva was ready to roll.

"Out! I want out!" Eva tugged at the strap holding her in place.

"We'll be there soon." She put her hand to stop the little girl from releasing the buckle. Eva knew how to get herself out of the car seat. Too bad Shelby hadn't been able to teach her yet how to get in on her own.

"I'm bored." Eva threw her head back to stare up at the ceiling. Then she looked at the snow. "Can we make a snowman?"

"Maybe later." Eva's disappointment brought a fresh wave of guilt. Was this her fault? If she had been more in tune as to what Emmitt was doing, could they have avoided being in the center of danger?

"There's a television at the new house," Aiden said helpfully.

"Don't care. I wanna build a snowman."

"Eva, behave." She used her stern teacher's voice. "You don't get to have everything you want."

Her daughter's lower lip trembled, but thankfully, they'd arrived at the safe house. The place appeared newer than the rental Brady had secured for them yesterday under Marc's name, the outside a brown brick with tan trim. The homes in this neighborhood were farther apart too.

But the best feature of all was the bulletproof windows.

"Ready?" Aiden asked.

"Yes." The driveway and sidewalks were not plowed or shoveled, so she'd have to carry Eva in. "Now you can get out of your car seat."

"Goody." The little girl made short work of the buckles.

"Hold on a minute," Shelby warned. "The snow is deep."

"I'll take her," Aiden offered.

Eva didn't seem to mind. The inside of the home was nice enough but impersonal. Even hotel rooms and rental properties had artwork or photos on the walls.

This place had nothing like that.

Aiden went back outside to shovel, leaving her to explore. It didn't take long for the rest of the family to trickle in.

"Shelby, this is Reed Carmichael, he's engaged to my twin, Alanna. This is my older sister, Kyleigh, and of course you know Tarin and Brady." Aiden gestured to each one as he introduced them. "This is Marc Callahan; he's also with the FBI."

"It's nice to meet you." She rested her hand on Eva's head. The little girl had turned shy with all the newcomers. "This is my daughter, Eva."

"It's nice to meet you," Reed and Marc said at the same time. Kyleigh laughed and came over to give her a hug. "I told Aiden I wanted to be here to level out the testosterone."

She smiled at Aiden's beautiful red-haired sister. If not

for the gun on her belt, Shelby would have assumed she was a model. "Tell me about it."

"Let's sit around the kitchen table," Aiden said. "We have a lot of work to do."

Heartened by the sheer strength in numbers, Shelby joined the Finnegans, feeling certain they'd come up with a strategy that would put an end to this nightmare very soon.

# CHAPTER NINE

"Let me start at the beginning since Reed and Kyleigh may not know what's been going on." Aiden took a moment to gather his thoughts. "While attending the funeral for Sergeant Major Gregory Savage, who is Shelby's father and Eva's grandfather, someone took a shot at them during the twenty-one-gun salute." He described how the frozen ground had kicked up and how they'd gotten out of there. "Then someone was waiting at Shelby's home and tried again. Then we were found at the American Lodge; I believe Gary verified there was a GPS tracker on her Jeep. Then we were discovered again outside the homestead while in Brady's car. The perp used a signal jammer to mess with our phones. We rented clean vehicles and headed out to the Timberland Falls Suites. I called Tom Mitchell, an army intelligence officer I know, and he came out to meet with us there. He let us know about a rumor related to Shelby's deceased husband, Emmitt Copeland, and the fact that he may have been having an extramarital affair. Tom and I thought maybe the current shooting might be related to that, for example, a family member of the female soldier found out and has come after Shelby seeking revenge. Or maybe that Shelby's father discovered something and put an end to someone's career. Tom brought a list of female soldiers including three who had been recently discharged from the National Guard."

His family members, or in Reed's case, almost family member, were listening with interest. He was grateful to have a group with so much experience on their side.

"Ninety minutes after Tom Mitchell left us at the hotel, he was shot," Aiden continued. "The long time frame is odd; we think he may have stopped for lunch. Thankfully, he managed to call and warn me so we could get out of the hotel. Which we did. But we later learned he died as a result of this so-called random shooting event."

"Random? Yeah, right," Reed muttered.

"Ditto," Marc Callahan said.

Aiden nodded. "I have only just started going through the list of names. I have a few names of women who may have had an affair with Emmitt, but I also found a woman by the name of Amy Golden who committed suicide three weeks ago."

"Interesting timing." Kyleigh looked thoughtful.

"Exactly." He glanced at Shelby, then said, "We were at a rental house when yet another shooter showed up. Thankfully, I saw him early enough that we could get out of there, but I have no idea how we were found. The property was rented under Marc Callahan's name, which makes me think someone with a lot of brass could be involved."

"That's not good," Tarin said with a frown.

"I double checked with Donovan, our special agent in charge," Brady said. "He spoke to a Sergeant Major Bill

Parsons who referred the new army investigator, Heath Strauss, to the case."

Marc scratched his chin. "You're thinking one of them dug up the connection between me, Brady, and Aiden? And what, came out themselves or hired a shooter?"

"That's my working theory, unless you can come up with another possibility." He spread his hands wide. "We ditched our smart phones. We're using a rental car and were staying in a rental property."

"True," Marc agreed. "But the army brass now knows the feds are involved, so maybe someone within the chain of command dug deep enough to find the link between the Callahans and Finnegans."

"Everyone at the grave site watched as Aiden took me and Eva away," Shelby spoke up. "It was no secret that Aiden was helping me."

"And it never occurred to me that our family connection is on a DNA website for anyone to see," Aiden admitted. "I should have thought of that."

"Either way, it seems highly likely that someone who is currently in the army is involved," Reed said. "Is the affair the only reason someone would come after Shelby and Eva?"

"I haven't been able to come up with another reason." He shrugged, then added, "But I'm open to suggestions."

"The woman who committed suicide is an angle we need to investigate further," Kyleigh said.

"We lost power last night in the storm, it came back on just as the bad guy showed up, so I haven't had time to do that yet." He frowned. "If Amy was having an affair, why would she kill herself now when Emmitt Copeland died two years ago?"

There was a long moment of silence as the group considered the possibilities.

"People in love do crazy things," Brady finally said. "Maybe she was depressed before the affair happened and hadn't been able to deal with it."

"Maybe." Aiden was no expert on behavioral health issues. "Keep in mind, I didn't get through the list. There are other names to look into. And there is no guarantee that we're on the right track. Mitchell was the one who mentioned hearing the rumors of an affair, but he was going to do more research and dig deeper into some key personnel files. Which brings us to the meeting that we're supposed to have with Lieutenant Heath Strauss, the guy replacing Mitchell."

"We need a neutral meeting ground," Reed agreed. "One that enables us to surround the place to protect Shelby and Eva."

"Yes, and the recent snowstorm will limit our outdoor possibilities." Tarin thought for a moment, then said, "We could use the American Lodge. Gary is always super supportive of us."

"I thought of that, but there's still only one way in and out of the rooms." Aiden grimaced. "I was thinking of another rental property."

"I can rent a place," Reed offered. "My last name shouldn't raise any red flags."

Aiden grinned at his soon-to-be brother-in-law. "I would appreciate that, thanks. Maybe find a place that's somewhat isolated to make it easier to surround the property."

Reed reached for the computer. "I'll start searching now."

"I have Heath Strauss's contact information," Brady

said. "But I think we should wait to call from the new rental property to keep this one secret."

"I like that idea," Shelby said. "It's been a long time since I've felt safe, the way I do here."

His heart ached for her. "I agree, this location needs to be kept highly confidential."

"It's nice." Marc glanced around with interest. "The bullet-resistant glass windows are a great feature."

"We've used it before," Tarin said. "Thankfully, my boss has been decent about allowing me to pay for the privilege of using it for our family's personal situations."

"We can chip in too," Kyleigh said. "I didn't realize it was coming out of your pocket, Tarin."

"Not a problem." Tarin waved that off. "Let's just focus on our next steps."

Eva began to fuss, so Shelby excused herself to take care of the little girl. He caught Kyleigh's curious gaze, as if she could see his interest. He did his best to stay cool, hoping she wouldn't say anything to embarrass him.

Or Shelby.

"I found a place," Reed announced. "It's located outside of Timberland Falls." He turned the computer to show the map. "No other homes nearby for a half-mile radius."

"Book it," Aiden said. "We'll need to get out there before making the call to Strauss."

"Should we keep Shelby and Eva here?" Marc asked.

"I considered that, but Strauss will likely want to talk to Shelby." Aiden glanced at Brady, who nodded.

"I agree. With so many of us, we can keep them safe." Brady grinned. "We'll need to draw straws to determine who has to stay outside."

"You all do," Tarin said. "I'm staying inside with Shelby, Eva, and Aiden. The rest of you are out on patrol."

"Oh yeah?" Marc raised a brow. "I'm the oldest. I think I should be the one staying inside."

"You're the oldest of the Callahan family, not ours," Kyleigh pointed out. "However, it may be smart to have a federal agent in on the meeting too. That way the army will know they can't mess around."

"Okay, fine. Brady will stay inside with Aiden, Shelby, and Eva." Tarin pinned the others with a narrow gaze. "We'll work together to keep them safe."

"Agreed," Reed said, waiting a moment for the others to silently nod in agreement. "The rental property is booked. We should head out now. It's about a forty-five-minute drive without taking the recent snowfall into consideration."

Aiden swept his gaze over his family. "I can't thank you enough for doing this."

"Hey, we're glad to help," Kyleigh said with a grin. "Let's hit the road. I think Reed should take the lead. Aiden, you follow him, and the rest of us will fall in behind. Once we reach the property, Reed, Marc, Tarin, and I will split up, covering each of the compass points."

"Sounds good." He was truly touched by how quickly they'd come running. He turned toward Shelby and Eva. "Ready to go?"

"No! Don't wanna!" Eva stamped her foot, her expression stubborn. She looked so cute he had to work hard not to laugh. Especially since Shelby appeared a bit frazzled.

"Oh, did I forget to give you another toy?" Brady said, feigning surprise.

Instantly, Eva's gaze locked on his. "You brought me a toy?"

"I did, but only good girls get toys." Brady put his hand in his pocket, regarding her steadily. "Good girls take car trips without complaining when their mommy needs to go someplace."

"I like car trips." Eva ran toward him. "I'll be good!"

"Okay." Brady pulled his hand from his pocket and handed her three farm toys. A cow, a goat, and a pig. "Do you know what these animals are?"

To Aiden's surprise, Eva knew them. She took the plastic animals from Brady, but then Shelby put a hand on her arm.

"What do you say to Mr. Brady?" Shelby prompted.

"Thank you." Eva barely looked at Brady, though; she was already making farm animal noises.

"Cute," Reed said with a smile. "I'll have to remember that trick."

"Yeah?" Tarin scowled. "You and Alanna just got engaged."

Reed arched a brow. "I'm aware."

"Give him a break, Tarin. Let's hit the road," Brady said.

Aiden packed the computer, figuring they'd have time to work while waiting for Strauss to arrive. Ten minutes later, they were back on the road in their caravan heading north to Timberland Falls.

He kept an eye on their rearview mirror out of sheer habit, not because he didn't trust his family to back him up.

"You think this will work?" Shelby asked.

"Yes." He glanced at her. "Are you worried?"

"Not really." A smile tugged at the corner of her mouth. "Having your family accompanying us makes a big difference."

"I feel the same way." He shrugged, then said, "I hope we can trust Strauss. Having someone on our side who can get the information we need is huge."

"I know." She sighed and tucked her hair behind her ear. "But really, how will we know? He could just pretend to be on our side, right? And then pull something sneaky when we least expect it?"

Since he'd had the same concern, he nodded. "He could be working for whoever is responsible. If so, the remote location of the property might work in our favor. Maybe he'll make a move today without having any clue just how much backup we have waiting in the wings."

"I guess that alone would put us on the right path," Shelby murmured. "Everyone in the army can't be responsible for this."

He didn't say anything. Someone high enough in the military ranks could set something up without the soldiers on the ground even knowing what was really going on. Carrying out orders without questioning them was the hardest part of his job. Questioning your superiors wasn't encouraged. At all.

The way it should be.

"What if this investigator is followed the same way Tom Mitchell was?"

"If he's taking over Tom's investigation, he'll know what happened and make sure he's not as vulnerable." He glanced at her. "Try not to worry. The army tends to take shootings seriously, especially when one of their own is taken out."

"They didn't seem too concerned when Emmitt died," she said.

He hesitated, choosing his words carefully. "Emmitt was killed during a riot. Those are some of the most dangerous situations we face. There's always a lot of chaos, and far too many civilians carry weapons. Tom said he investigated your husband's death and deemed it accidental. We have to trust he did a thorough job."

She nodded, her expression grim, but didn't say anything more. He understood how difficult this was for her. First losing her husband, then her father, then discovering her husband's infidelity.

Not to mention being shot at more times than he cared to count.

His phone rang. He answered Reed's call. "Are we getting close?"

"Yep. See that white farmhouse? That's our destination."

"Looks good." He remembered seeing the image on the computer. "There are trees along the northwest side but open fields to the east."

"I can cover the east without a problem," Reed assured him. "I have a white sweatshirt with me."

He winced. "You're going to get wet."

"Won't be the first time," Reed drawled. "That's my problem, not yours."

"Thanks." If Aiden didn't know better, he'd assume Reed was only doing this to get in his good graces because of being in love with his twin sister. But he'd discovered Reed was a genuinely nice guy.

He should have known Alanna wouldn't have loved the guy if he wasn't honest, decent, and true.

It occurred to him that his twin would not be happy if he allowed Reed to get hurt during this plan of theirs.

He said a silent prayer. *Please, Lord Jesus, keep us all safe in Your care.*

"THE HOUSE LOOKS HUGE." Shelby turned to look at Aiden. "We're only staying here until we finish meeting with Lieutenant Strauss, right?"

"Right." He reached for her hand. She found herself gripping it tightly, unwilling to let go. In the back seat, Eva was singing "Old MacDonald Had a Farm," while moving the farm animals up and down as if they were dancing. Thank goodness for Brady knowing it didn't take much to distract a three-year-old. "Once we know it's safe, we'll return to the original safe house Tarin arranged for us."

"Okay." She tried to smile, swallowing against a knot of nerves. "Nothing against the farmhouse, but it doesn't look as bulletproof as the other place."

"We chose this place so we could make sure no one was able to sneak up to take another shot at you." He gently squeezed her hand. "The gunman won't get close enough to shoot through any windows."

"I know." She blew out a breath and forced a smile. Aiden was doing his best. Not just Aiden, but his family too. "Ironic that the one who avoided the military is now in the cross hairs of a killer."

"Do you regret marrying Emmitt?"

What? Where had that question come from? "No." She turned to glance back at Eva. "I could never regret Eva. She's worth everything."

He nodded. "She is. And you should know I think Emmitt was an idiot."

The added comment almost made her smile for real. Up ahead, Reed slowed his speed, using his blinker to indicate the driveway of the rental house, then continued on, driving past. She wasn't sure where he planned to park the car, then figured it wouldn't matter. Aiden turned into the freshly plowed driveway. Apparently, whoever owned the place had hired people to help take care of upkeep, which was a good thing because the snow seemed even deeper out here.

She told herself there was no reason to worry about his siblings and cousin Marc. They were all well-trained cops and FBI agents who could take care of themselves.

When Aiden slowed and began to turn around in the driveway, she had a flashback to how they'd barreled out of the garage earlier that morning without even waiting for the garage door to get all the way up. This driveway was longer, but the ability to drive straight out, rather than backing up, was probably a good way to ensure they were able to escape if needed.

She wasn't surprised when Brady pulled in behind them and did the same thing. She quickly pushed open her passenger-side door. Aiden joined her.

"I can carry her," he offered.

"Thanks." She unbuckled the little girl.

"Now can we make as snowman?" Eva asked.

"Not yet." Aiden glanced at her with a hint of panic. Shelby could tell he wasn't used to saying no to young children. She had to admit, it wasn't easy to hold the line when Eva gazed up at her with bright, adorable eyes. "Maybe later."

"Not later, now," Eva said with a pout.

"Don't forget your farm animals." Shelby picked the cow up from where Eva had dropped it on the seat. "Wasn't that nice of Mr. Brady to bring you toys?"

Eva nodded. "I like Mr. Brady."

"Ouch," Aiden muttered. "No loyalty with this one."

"Yeah, I'm afraid she's fickle." Shelby chuckled and followed him up to the house. He shifted Eva to one arm, then unlocked the keypad.

The farmhouse wasn't quite as clean as the pictures

made it look, but it was certainly large with windows on all sides. The kitchen was bright and recently renovated with white cupboards and a solid granite surface. There was a smaller in-room kitchen dinette set, along with a large dining room in the next room. Since they weren't staying, she decided there was no point in checking out the bedrooms.

If all went according to plan, they would only be here for a couple of hours at the most.

Brady came inside, stomping snow from his boots. "Okay, Aiden. Call Strauss."

Why she held her breath as he did so, she had no idea. He didn't put the call on speaker, but she listened to his side of the conversation.

"Lieutenant Strauss? This is Staff Sergeant Finnegan. Ms. Copeland and I would love to meet with you as soon as possible."

Aiden caught and held her gaze reassuringly, even as he listened.

"Eleven thirty is fine. I'll give you the address to where we're staying." He rattled off the information, then added, "Lieutenant Tom Mitchell was followed and murdered. I hope you take precautions. Whoever is behind these shooting attempts won't hesitate to eliminate anyone who gets in his or her way."

Another silence. She glanced at Brady, who was also listening while texting on his phone. She assumed he was providing the rest of the team information on the proposed timeline.

She checked her watch surprised to find it was already nine forty-five. Less than two hours until Strauss was scheduled to arrive.

"Yes, sir. I appreciate your concern. Trust me, we've barely

managed to stay ahead of the shooter ourselves. See you soon."
Aiden lowered the phone and looked at her. "We're set."

"I heard. Eleven thirty." She frowned. "Do you know
where he's coming from? Milwaukee? Madison? Green
Bay?"

"Madison." Aiden shrugged. "Soldiers are scattered all
over the state, but the Army National Guard base is outside
of Madison."

"That's at least an hour away, maybe more," Brady
pointed out.

"I know. Unfortunately, there's nothing I can do about
that." Aiden looked chagrined. "I feel bad Marc, Tarin,
Kyleigh, and Reed will be stuck out there for so long."

"They can handle it," Brady said. "We would do it for
them, too, if the situation was reversed."

"I'm going to see what I can find on TV for Eva." She
turned toward the living room. The furniture itself was
comfortable enough but not new like the kitchen. The television was the same brand she had at home, so it didn't take
long to find another cartoon.

Eva sat on the floor, surrounded by her dolly, trucks,
cars, and farm animals. For a moment, she gazed at her
daughter, her heart constricting painfully in her chest.

She could never regret marrying Emmitt and having
been blessed with Eva. But every time she thought about his
infidelity, she felt sick to her stomach. How could she have
been so naïve? So clueless?

Forcing the wave of self-doubt and recrimination aside,
she returned to the kitchen to find Aiden making coffee.

"Need help?"

"Nope." He flashed a smile. "Have a seat. We'll be here
for a while."

Brady's phone rang. "My boss," he said, before lifting the phone to his ear. "Donovan? Yeah, we're set. The meeting with Lieutenant Strauss will be at eleven thirty."

She wanted to ask why there weren't more FBI agents involved but held back. She should be grateful they had two feds and three cops, in addition to Aiden.

Six against one. There was no reason to be nervous. She swallowed hard and tried to relax.

The Finnegans were the strongest family she'd ever known. Not just in their chosen careers but also in their faith. She felt safe and secure in their care.

Aiden brought her a cup of coffee, complete with nondairy creamer and sugar the way she liked it. She curled her fingers around the hot mug, cradling it gratefully. "Thank you."

"You're welcome." His low, husky voice made her shiver.

"Don't worry about me," Brady said with a lopsided smile. "I can get my own."

"Yep, you can." Aiden ignored his older brother's dig and dropped into the chair beside her. "Patience is a virtue, right?"

"Right." She managed a smile.

The next hour passed with excruciating slowness. It was worse than when they'd waited for Mitchell to show because she was all too aware of the others hiding outside in the cold.

Brady abruptly straightened, holding up his phone. "Looks like our guy might be early. Reed thinks he's here but drove past as if to check the place out."

"Oh yeah?" Aiden stood and moved to the window overlooking the street. "At least he's being careful."

She shifted her gaze from Aiden to Brady and back to Aiden. "Why is he early? To catch us off guard?"

"Could be the traffic wasn't as bad as he'd anticipated." Aiden shrugged, then said, "I'm not surprised. I expected him to show up early."

She stood and crossed to the doorway leading into the living room. Eva was lying on the sofa now watching her cartoon with sleepy eyes.

"He's back." Aiden's voice drew her back to the kitchen.

"I'm sure he has no idea we have the place surrounded," Brady said.

"I agree." Aiden continued to watch from the window. "He returned too quickly to have made a more thorough search."

"I hope he did a better job of watching for a tail," Brady muttered, his fingers working his phone. She sat back at the table, waiting anxiously.

Aiden moved from the window to open the door. He stood back to let Lieutenant Strauss enter the farmhouse. He was dressed in a formal uniform, and his gaze narrowed when he saw Brady standing near Aiden.

"Staff Sergeant Finnegan? You didn't mention there would be anyone else here."

"You didn't ask." Aiden shut the door. "This is my brother, FBI Agent Brady Finnegan. And this is Ms. Copeland. She's the one who has been targeted by gunfire nonstop over the past forty-eight hours."

She rose on shaky legs to shake Lieutenant Strauss's hand. The lieutenant nodded at Brady, then turned back to Aiden. "I don't like being ambushed. There was no mention of the FBI being here."

"My brother has my back," Aiden said firmly. "Something I haven't gotten from the army recently."

After a long tense moment, the investigator shrugged. "Okay. Considering how Mitchell was killed, I can understand you taking extra precautions. Let's sit down and get to work."

Shelby sank back into her seat. So far, so good.

Maybe, just maybe this guy was on their side after all.

# CHAPTER TEN

Lieutenant Strauss sat down, then pulled a computer from a slim bag. Aiden sat on one side, while Brady sat on the other. Shelby was across from them. He gave her a hopefully reassuring smile, then waited for Strauss to begin.

"I walked the area where Mitchell was shot." Strauss turned his computer toward him. Aiden leaned forward to examine the map. "This area here"—he tapped the screen—"is likely the position from where the shooter waited."

"This is roughly six miles from the hotel." Seeing the close proximity for himself was sobering. "That means Mitchell had to have stopped for lunch first before heading out. And once he was hit, he called to warn us. We were able to escape before the shooter got down from his perch, then drove to the hotel."

"Is this your cell number?" Strauss recited a series of digits matching those of his disposable phone.

"Yes."

Strauss turned the computer back so he could make notes. "We found a receipt for a family restaurant, which matches your theory on where he was prior to hitting the road. How long was Mitchell with you?"

He glanced at Shelby, thinking back. "Less than an hour. Maybe forty-five minutes?"

She nodded in agreement.

"Here's what doesn't make sense." Strauss sat back in his chair, pinning him with a narrow gaze. "If Mitchell was followed to your hotel, why not ambush him there? The shooter could have taken all three of you out at one time."

"Four of us," Shelby swiftly interjected. "My three-year-old daughter was with us."

Strauss nodded. "You're right. Although it's difficult to know for certain if your daughter would have been killed, too, or simply left behind as not being a threat."

Just the thought of Eva watching her mother be shot and killed and left alone with her body was enough to make his stomach churn. "Neither option is acceptable."

"I didn't mean to insinuate it was," Strauss said. "But I still think the shooter's decision-making isn't logical. He could have shot Mitchell at the hotel, or at the restaurant. But didn't strike out until he was on the road."

Aiden had to admit the guy was right.

Brady spoke up. "Could the shooter have keyed into Mitchell's cell phone or vehicle GPS? Maybe he was on the way to the hotel, but before he could get to Timberland Falls, he discovered Mitchell left. He didn't realize the guy was going to stay for lunch, leaving him little choice but to wait to ambush him? Fewer witnesses to alert the police if he took the shot on a busy highway."

Strauss looked thoughtful. "That's one possible scenario."

"If that is what happened, only someone with high military access could have gotten that level of information,"

Aiden said. "The shooter is not a boots-on-the-ground soldier."

Strauss nodded. "I can look into whether or not Ms. Copeland's father made any enemies that might explain this."

"Even if my father made someone angry, I don't see why they'd track me and Eva down to shoot us." Shelby scowled. "Tom thought these attacks were personal. Which is why he was thinking my husband's infidelity was at the center of this."

"I read the notes Tom sent prior to his murder." Strauss tapped the keyboard. "He mentioned a list of female soldiers and something about running a report on any disciplinary action taken by Sergeant Major Savage."

"We thought Shelby's father may have uncovered the truth about Copeland's affair and took action against the female soldier involved," Aiden said.

Strauss grimaced. "Well, I'm sorry to disappoint you, but I could not find any disciplinary actions by Savage against a female soldier for the past three years. I didn't go back any farther because I didn't want us to head down the wrong path."

He locked gazes with Shelby. "Well, that's not helpful."

"I'm sorry." Strauss shrugged. "Any other ideas?"

Aiden had hoped this guy would come with more theories and intel. "Mitchell said he couldn't prove Copeland had an affair. He had planned to reinterview soldiers working alongside him to see if they cough up a name now that Shelby and Eva are in danger. Are you able to do that too?"

"Yes. But I'd like to put in a request for another search first," Strauss said. "We've mentioned upper brass being involved. I've requested a list of senior officers who have daughters in the National Guard."

He could see how a father could be irate about an affair. "Do you really think someone with bars and stars would attempt to shoot an innocent woman and child for something her husband had done?"

"I think we need to consider any and all possibilities," Strauss said.

"It can't hurt." Brady shrugged. "I mean, that list can't be that long, right?"

"Wait, that reminds me." Aiden dug out the list of female soldiers he'd been investigating. "You should check on this woman, Amy Golden. She committed suicide three weeks ago."

Strauss whistled. "Now that is a powerful motive."

As the investigator attacked the keyboard, Aiden caught Brady's gaze, silently asking if they should have their backup come inside out of the cold. From what he could tell, Strauss wasn't the leak. He seemed intent on getting to the bottom of Mitchell's murder.

Brady gave an imperceptible nod, then sent a text to the group.

"Amy Golden does not have a father, mother, or brother in the army," Strauss announced.

"What about having family in some other branch of law enforcement?" Aiden asked. "Same rules apply."

"I can look into that." Brady glanced up from his phone and gave an imperceptible shake of his head. Aiden took that to mean the team outside intended to stay put for a while. Mitchell said, "I'll call my boss."

"That would be great." If Strauss noticed Brady's texting, he didn't mention it. "Did you happen to find anything else interesting from the list?"

"Yes, but nothing that can be used as proof of an affair." Aiden showed him the pictures of female soldiers. Strauss's eyebrows levered upward when he saw Justine's photo.

"That name rings a bell." Strauss went back to working the keyboard. "Oh yeah, here it is. She filed sexual harassment charges against Sergeant Oliver Kennedy."

"Kennedy?" Aiden frowned. "He was at Shelby's father's funeral as a pallbearer. He was near us, though, so he couldn't have made the shot."

Strauss grimaced. "So likely not involved."

"I can't see how a sexual harassment charge against Oliver Kennedy would result in someone shooting at Shelby and her daughter."

"Maybe not, but you may be on the right track," Brady said. "What about any sexual assault allegations against Emmitt Copeland?"

"I believe that was reviewed back when he was killed, but I'll double check." Strauss tapped more keys. "Nothing was filed against Copeland." The investigator looked at Shelby for a moment as if feeling guilty about having these frank discussions about her dead husband.

"It could be that the charges were going to be filed, but then Emmitt was shot, so there was no point," Brady said thoughtfully. "It might be wise to interview Justine Brooks to see if what she has to say about Emmitt Copeland."

"This is going to take too long." Shelby's outburst startled him. "We have been in constant danger. Interviews, poking into every possible woman who might have a grudge against Emmitt could take days, even weeks." She crossed her arms defensively over her chest. "I have to go back to work on Monday."

"I would advise against that," Strauss said.

"You need to find who is behind this!" She jabbed her finger at the investigator.

Aiden wanted to reassure her that they'd figure this out, but he understood her frustration. He and his family had kept her safe without much help from the army. Except for Tom Mitchell who'd been shot for his efforts.

"You're right, Ms. Copeland. We do need to get this shooter behind bars." Strauss sighed and rubbed the back of his neck. "I will put in a request for MPs to keep you and your daughter safe."

"Don't bother," Aiden said in a curt tone. "I don't trust anyone within the army right now, and we've been doing okay on our own."

"I agree with Aiden. I don't want anyone else assigned to watch over me," Shelby added. "Why can't you just find this person and arrest him?"

Strauss looked chagrined. "I will do my best."

Shelby bit her lower lip and turned away as if holding back yet another retort.

He didn't blame Shelby for venting her frustration. She had every right to be upset about what the army had or hadn't done. He turned to Strauss. "How long will it take for the army to get you the information on the list of senior officers with daughters in the military?"

In answer, Strauss went back to his computer. "I guess we'll find out."

It was his turn to swallow a wave of frustration. That answer wasn't good enough either, but there was no easy way to cut through the red tape that the military was famous for. Especially when it came to getting intel on the upper brass.

In that moment, he found it difficult to imagine staying within the Army National Guard. Working his way up the ranks didn't hold the same appeal as it once had. Obviously, senior officers deserved to be treated with the respect their rank deserved.

But they did not have the right to hide behind their bars and stars to commit crimes either.

"Mommy!" Shelby sent him a helpless glance as she jumped up from her seat at the table to tend to her daughter.

"They don't deserve this," Aiden said in a low voice. "You better get the access you need and fast."

"I know." Strauss looked just as grim. "I don't believe Mitchell was taken seriously when he broached the idea of someone within the army being involved in the attempted murder of a civilian. Now I think the army understands this has the power to blow up in their face."

"And that's why the FBI intends to work the case with you," Brady pointed out. "I have to be honest, I'm still sitting here trying to decide if we should trust you."

Strauss arched a brow. "Is that why you have someone outside watching the place?"

Aiden had to admit, the guy was good. "You knew?"

"I saw one person and figured you had called in some backup." Strauss nodded to the other room where Shelby was talking softly to Eva. "I can understand why. They don't deserve this."

Brady held the investigator's gaze. "Four officers. Not one."

This time, Strauss looked shocked. "Really?"

"Can we get back to the matter at hand?" Aiden asked. "I can keep going down this list of female officers, but we also need to see a list of those who were discharged, honorably or not, within the past three years too. Mitchell only went back two years."

"That I can get easily enough." Strauss tapped a few keys. "The army doesn't care as much about those soldiers who have left the military and turned civilian."

"Separate it by gender," he suggested. "We should probably start with the women."

"Will do." He watched the screen for a moment, then nodded. "We have three women and ten men."

Sensing the army investigator planned to stay awhile, he shot another questioning look at Brady. Strauss had been there for a solid hour, and Kyleigh, Marc, Reed, and Tarin had to be chilled to the bone.

Brady nodded and stood. "Excuse me." His brother left the room, pulling out his phone as he walked.

"How have you been searching on the female soldiers?" Strauss asked.

"Just through social media," he acknowledged. "I had hoped the army would provide some intel too."

"They for sure have the basics, name, address, phone number, and serial numbers," Strauss said. "That will need to be cross-referenced with other databases. It's not as easy as it looks on TV."

"Can you do that here? With the laptop?"

"Yep." Strauss didn't look up from the screen. "But I will still need to input one name at a time."

Brady returned a minute later. He flashed his phone screen so that Aiden could see the text from Tarin saying they would stay put for a while longer. He nodded, thinking his family was really going out on a limb for them.

"I started with Amy Golden," Strauss said. "There's nothing in her background that raises any red flags. Her file states that there was no known reason for her suicide."

"Meaning they weren't aware of a sexual assault or other crime that may have driven her over the edge." Aiden frowned. "She wouldn't have been the first female soldier to have had such an allegation ignored by her superior."

"True, but according to the report, she hadn't confided in anyone about such an event either. Not to her friends, or her family." Strauss sighed. "Without anything more to go on, we should move onto the next possible suspect."

"Just because it's not in the report doesn't mean it didn't happen," Aiden argued. "Who did that investigation?"

"Tom Mitchell." Strauss looked surprised. "I believe he'd have dug deep."

"Yeah." More frustration hit hard. This wasn't going to be an easy road. Not when it seemed they hit a wall at every turn.

Brady abruptly looked up from his phone. "Hey. We have company."

Aiden instantly leaped up and ran to the next room. "Shelby, grab your coat and Eva's too."

"What's going on?" Her eyes were wide with alarm, but she thankfully did as he'd asked. Eva protested, but he ignored her.

"Someone is coming." He swept the little girl into his arms and ushered Shelby into the kitchen. "Brady? Can we drive out of here?"

"Reed is asking that we go into the basement." Brady swept the computers off the table, tucking them under his arm. "Let's go."

"What? Why?" Strauss looked alarmed, as if realizing for the first time the magnitude of the danger.

It was all Aiden could do not to yell at the guy. The only way they could have been found is if someone had tracked the investigator to this location.

THE BASEMENT WAS DARK, damp, and generally awful. Shelby knew she shouldn't have expected anything different. It was an old farmhouse after all.

"I'm scared." Eva buried her face against Aiden's neck. He cradled her daughter close for a moment, murmuring words of encouragement before transferring Eva into her arms.

"I need to be able to shoot if necessary," he whispered.

She nodded in understanding. "You're not going to leave us here, are you?"

"Not yet." Aiden and Brady exchanged a long look. "Brady is going up to stand guard in the kitchen."

Brady thrust the computers at Heath Strauss. "Stash these someplace safe."

"There's really someone out there?" Strauss asked.

"Yeah." Aiden stepped forward, his expression grim. "I don't think you were tailed, since you've been here for over an hour. But somehow you were tracked anyway."

"The same way Tom Mitchell was," Strauss said quietly. He set the computers over where an ancient-looking washer and dryer were located. "This is unbelievable."

"Now do you believe someone high in the ranks is behind this?" Aiden pulled his weapon and stood to one side of the bottom of the basement steps. "Take a post on the other side. I expect you to guard Shelby and Eva with your life if necessary."

"I will." To his credit, the investigator fell into position. Her gaze darted between the two men. Was it possible the shooter could get past their backup and into the house?

*Please, Lord! Please keep us all safe!*

Aiden gave her a nod as if understanding her whispered prayer. She lowered into a sitting position in front of the washer and dryer, resting her back against the appliances, then cradled Eva in her lap. From her position, she couldn't see the top of the stairs. Which was okay because she knew Aiden and Heath Strauss wouldn't let an intruder get very far.

Humbling to realize every single man and woman located inside and outside the house would not hesitate to put their lives on the line for her.

And Eva.

The fact that it was necessary still messed with her mind. She inwardly railed against Emmitt for putting her and their daughter in this situation. Because the more she thought about these attacks being personal, the more convinced she was that he was the driving force behind them.

For long minutes, there was nothing but silence. It was difficult to sit there doing nothing while imagining what Kyleigh, Tarin, Marc, and Reed were dealing with.

"Do you really have four officers stationed outside?" Strauss asked in a low whisper.

Aiden glanced at him, but then turned his attention to the top of the stairs. "Yes, four members of my family are out there. Heaven help you, Strauss, if I discover you're part of this."

"I'm not!" There was a hint of panic in the guy's tone. "I would never hurt innocent people."

"Then who would?" Aiden shot back. "Think fast because you're a target now as much as we are."

"I wish I knew." The investigator's tone was laced with bitterness. "Trust me, I was not expecting this."

"Yeah, you can see why I don't trust you," Aiden muttered.

The two men fell silent again, and Shelby could tell

the not knowing about what was going on outside was wearing on Aiden's nerves. She may have only known him for a few days, but she understood he would far rather be stationed on the front lines than relegated to the basement.

A gunshot rang out, followed by two more staccato shots.

Aiden and Strauss didn't move, their weapons trained on the doorway at the top of the steps. Shelby glanced around, looking for something, anything she could use as a weapon. But there was nothing other than a very dusty bottle of laundry detergent.

"Everyone okay down there?" Brady called.

"Yes. What about the others?" Aiden asked.

"Hold tight. I see one perp down." Brady sounded calm, as if this was something that happened every day. Or maybe he had that much faith in the four officers that had offered to back them up.

What would have happened if they hadn't stayed outside standing guard? She shivered, knowing things could have gone much differently.

"All clear!" Brady called. She closed her eyes and pressed her cheek to Eva's hair.

"Shelby?" Aiden crossed over to her side. "Can I help with Eva?"

"Yes." Her voice came out in a croak, her throat thick with pent-up tears. Thankfully, Eva didn't put up a fight as Aiden took the little girl from her.

Rising on shaky knees, she followed Aiden upstairs. There was no sign of Brady. When she looked outside, she saw everyone except Aiden and Heath Strauss outside, surrounding a man lying on the ground.

"Get the computers up here," Aiden directed. "We're

going to want to try to identify this guy and may need to do a search in the army database."

Strauss nodded and did as he asked. She stepped up beside Aiden, who slipped his arm around her waist.

"We're safe," he said in a low voice.

"Thanks to you and your family," she whispered.

A crooked smile creased his features. "I told you we'd manage without help from the army."

"You did." She allowed herself the luxury of leaning against him, soaking in his strength. How many times had Aiden saved her life?

Too many.

"Hey, don't cry," he said when she sniffled. "We're okay. And this could end up being a break in the case. The danger could be over for good."

She lifted her head to glance up at him. "You think so?" The way her daughter rested against Aiden made her heart ache. Emmitt had thrown this away, and for what? The thrill of a sordid affair?

"We'll find out." He smiled and surprised her with a sweet but potent kiss. Only when Strauss clattered back up the stairs did he lift his head. "Soon, I hope."

It wasn't easy, but she stepped back, putting some distance between them. She could feel Strauss's curious gaze on them. Yet she also couldn't bring herself to care what he thought of her feelings for Aiden.

"I'll, uh, head outside." Strauss set one laptop on the table.

"Hold on, Strauss." Aiden held up a hand, as Brady turned and glanced at the house. "Looks like my brother may already have an ID on the shooter."

Less than fifteen seconds later, Brady stepped inside.

His gaze swept over her, Aiden, and Eva before coming to rest on Strauss. "Tim Tobin."

"Who?" Strauss looked confused.

"The wounded soldier is Tim Tobin." Brady's gaze narrowed. "His name hasn't come up in any of your investigations?"

"No. I've never heard of the guy." Setting the computer on the table, Strauss opened it and began typing. After a moment, he said, "Tobin enlisted in the army four years ago and has recently been honorably discharged from service after completing his four-year stint."

"What?" Aiden scowled. "You're saying this guy is a civilian?"

"Yes, exactly." Strauss typed more, apparently doing another search. A long minute later, he shook his head. "He does not have a parent or sibling who is still an active member of the military either."

Aiden looked frustrated. "Brady, how badly is he hurt?"

"Reed fired two rounds, hitting him twice in the abdomen a split second after the guy took a shot at him. He's moaning in pain and refusing to answer any questions."

"Ambulance on the way?" Aiden asked.

"Yes." Five seconds later, the wail of police sirens could be heard getting louder and louder as they approached the farmhouse.

"I don't understand how Tim Tobin, an ex-army soldier, had the resources needed to track me here." Strauss scowled.

Aiden and Brady exchanged another long look. "Someone hired him to do the job," Aiden finally said. Then he handed Shelby Eva and took a step closer to Strauss. "Convince me it wasn't you."

"I can't prove a negative," Strauss shot back. But Aiden didn't respond. A palpable tension shimmered between the two men. Finally, the investigator put his arms out, holding his wrists together. "You want to arrest me? Go ahead. But I'm telling you, I'm not involved in this."

Shelby wasn't sure what to believe. But her hope of this nightmare ending faded.

It seemed they were no closer to uncovering the truth.

# CHAPTER ELEVEN

It was very tempting to throw a set of handcuffs around Strauss's wrists, but deep down, Aiden's gut told him Heath wasn't the leak. The guy had appeared genuinely shocked to hear someone was approaching the place. Yet Aiden really didn't like the fact that they'd been found at the farmhouse.

Thank goodness they hadn't sacrificed the location of their safe house.

"I don't think we have probable cause to arrest him," Brady pointed out mildly, reading his mind.

He sighed and took a step back. "Yeah, I know. But we need to figure out how this keeps happening. How the gunman always finds us."

"I don't like being targeted any more than you do," Strauss said, his tone curt. "Maybe it's time we look at the guy who sent me here, Sergeant Major Bill Parsons."

"What do you know about him?" Brady asked.

"I've only been reporting to him for the past year, so unfortunately not much." Strauss grimaced. "The guy doesn't invite small talk and isn't very personable either."

"Not helpful," Aiden said.

Strauss sent him a sidelong glance. "I understand why you're ticked. I am too. But I didn't do this. Give me some time to see what I can uncover about Parsons."

"We can't stay here," Aiden said. "And I don't trust you enough to bring you to our safe house."

"Aiden." Brady rested a hand on his shoulder. "We can't leave him here or let him hang in the wind to end up like Tom Mitchell."

His brother was right. But that didn't mean he liked it. "We need to take precautions, then."

"That's reasonable." Brady turned toward Strauss. "We'll start by you shutting down your phone."

"The computer too," Aiden said. "That can be tracked just as easily as a phone."

Wordlessly, Strauss powered down his phone and the computer. "The only problem is that I can't investigate Bill Parsons without access to the army database."

He turned to his brother. "Can the feds help with that?"

"I'll talk to Ian, our tech guru. See what he can do to provide a computer that can't be easily traced." Brady turned toward the door as squads pulled into the long driveway. "Hopefully, we won't be stuck here too long."

"You and Marc are federal agents. Just pull rank," Aiden called out.

Brady shot him a sly grin over his shoulder without responding.

"I assume we'll have to give statements?" Shelby asked, frowning as officers and EMTs swarmed the area.

"I'm afraid so. But as soon as that's finished, we'll be able to leave." Aiden smiled reassuringly.

Eva squirmed in Shelby's arms, so she set the little girl

on the floor. "Come play wif me," she said, tugging on Shelby's hand.

"Go watch TV, okay?" Shelby's smile was strained. The little girl ran into the next room, seemingly unfazed by the commotion.

"I guess it's good she's resilient," Strauss murmured. The investigator turned toward Aiden. "Listen, I know you don't trust me, but I will do everything possible to figure out who is behind this. Targeting an innocent woman and child is heinous."

Aiden nodded. "No argument from me. But that was your mission from the beginning, wasn't it?"

"Yes, but I was specifically ordered to dig into the death of Tom Mitchell." Strauss frowned. "And now the exact same thing almost happened here. A random shooting. If you didn't have so much backup stationed outside . . ."

"And that's exactly why I did." Aiden softened his attitude toward the investigator. Looking back, he could tell the shock on the guy's face had been real. Besides, his brother was right. They needed help from inside the army. They needed Strauss. Probably as much as he needed them to help protect him. "And why I picked a neutral location for our meeting. I just wish we had more to go on than an injured former soldier by the name of Tim Tobin."

"There must be a way to link Tobin to the person who hired him." Strauss glanced at the laptop computer, then frowned. "It feels like we're fighting with both hands tied behind our backs."

A sharp knock at the door snagged his attention. He exchanged a look with Shelby, then crossed over to let the Timberland police officer inside.

"I don't care if the FBI has jurisdiction over this case, I want to know what's going on in my city." The officer's last name was Chester. "Which of you is Lieutenant Heath Strauss?"

Heath stepped forward and held out his badge identifying him as an army investigator. "I'm working with the FBI on the murder of my predecessor, Thomas Mitchell. He was shot and killed not far from here."

Chester frowned. "I remember, it was a drive-by shooting on the highway."

"Yes, and now another shooter crawled out of the woodwork." Heath's tone held a note of sarcasm. "Tim Tobin is former army, recently honorably discharged."

The cop's eyes narrowed. "Supposedly Tobin fired first, yet I find it interesting that he suffered two bullets to the gut."

"That's what happens when you fire at a cop when there are other cops backing you up." Aiden's comment drew Chester's attention. "Reed Carmichael is an officer with the MPD, and Kyleigh is with the Milwaukee County Sheriff's department. Tarin is a detective with the MPD too. You already know Brady Finnegan and Marc Callahan are with the FBI."

"Lots of firepower here for this little meeting." Chester glanced suspiciously between him and Heath. "Care to expand on what this is really about?"

Aiden sent Heath a warning glance not to say too much. But he needn't have worried.

"You do remember Mitchell was shot and killed, right?" Strauss arched a brow. "Did you think I wouldn't come prepared this time? I have no interest in being murdered, which is exactly what almost happened."

After a long moment, Officer Chester turned away. "Next time, pick a different city for your meeting. I don't want to be called to the scene of another shooting, understand?"

Heath glanced at him as if asking if this guy was for real. Aiden shrugged. "We understand and will take your request under advisement."

"Get out of here," Chester muttered harshly as he opened the door to head back outside. The cold November wind blew the door shut behind him.

"Your brother must have done some fast talking," Heath said. "I figured we'd be stuck here for hours."

"There are times it's good to be a Finnegan." He met the investigator's gaze. "I want to trust you, but if I find out you're playing against us? We'll bury you."

"No need for threats," Heath shot back. "I'm well aware of how close we came to being silenced forever."

"Enough already," Shelby said, sounding weary. "I don't think Heath is involved, and you heard the officer. We need to get out of here." She shot a sour glance around the farmhouse. "I won't miss this place."

Aiden understood the only place Shelby felt secure was at their safe house. He peered through the window. "Looks like the Timberland Falls cops are leaving."

"We need an update on Tobin's condition," Heath said.

He shrugged. "Too early to do that yet. Either Marc or Brady will follow up once we're out of here."

"How do we know Tobin came alone?" Shelby crossed her arms over her chest. "There could be another shooter out there."

"Reed, Kyleigh, Tarin, and Marc have secured the property." Yet he hated to admit she had a point. Heath had just pointed out how Mitchell was killed on the highway not far from here. And on his way back from their hotel. "I'll work something out with the family; there must be an alternative route back to Milwaukee."

Shelby nodded, her gaze reflecting her concern.

Tarin, Brady, Marc, Kyleigh, and Reed crowded into the kitchen. Reed was shivering, his sweatshirt soaked through from being stretched out on the snow and quickly nuked a cup of coffee to warm up. After a brief discussion, they agreed to head northeast, making a wide loop to return back to their original safe house.

"I'll lead the way," Reed offered, taking a sip of his coffee. "Worked well enough on the ride here."

Alanna would kill him if anything happened to her fiancé, but he nodded, grateful for his future brother-in-law's assistance.

"I promised to stick around here to help smooth things over with Timberland Falls PD," Tarin said. "Rhy would expect me to do that."

Aiden nodded. "Okay, Heath will ride with me, Shelby, and Eva," he said. "I don't want to risk him using his vehicle as it could be tracked via GPS. Brady, I need you, Kyleigh, and Marc to cover us from behind."

"Happy to," Brady said as Kyleigh and Marc nodded.

"Stay here while we get our vehicles out of hiding." Reed glanced at Strauss. "We'll park yours inside the barn since we're leaving it behind. May as well make some effort to hide it from view."

"Yeah, sure." Heath didn't look thrilled at leaving the vehicle behind, but he didn't voice a protest either. "Whatever you think is best."

"I'll get Eva ready to go," Shelby murmured, turning to head into the living room.

There was a long silence before Heath asked, "You really think this is related to her deceased husband?"

"All I know for sure is that it's something personal." He shrugged. "Like I said before, I'm open to other theories."

"This is really messed up," Heath muttered.

"Yeah." He could only nod in agreement.

Another fifteen minutes passed before all the vehicles were ready to go. Shelby insisted on riding in the back with Eva. The little girl balked at going for another car ride, but Shelby managed to coerce her daughter into climbing inside by using her toys.

Despite their convoy, Aiden was tense as they left the scene of the shooting behind. Going northeast would add at least a half hour to their trip, but taking extra time to stay safe was worth every minute.

Shelby did a good job of keeping Eva occupied until the little girl announced she was hungry. Since the hour was one thirty in the afternoon, he could understand why.

"Shelby, call Brady. Ask him to peel off to pick up lunch for everyone." Aiden met her gaze in the rearview mirror. "You can tell him what to get for Eva."

She nodded and did as he'd asked, then went back to playing with the dolly and farm animals. Eva grew tired of the game, though, and squirmed in her seat.

"Down! I wanna get down." The little girl began to unbuckle the strap of her car seat.

"Soon, sweetheart." Shelby brushed her hands out of the way. "You know the rule. You can't get out of the car seat while we're riding."

By the time they reached the safe house, Shelby was frazzled, and he wasn't doing much better. Being on the run with a small child made things that much more difficult. The good news was that there had been no attempt to shoot at them during their convoluted ride home, and Brady had brought several bags of fast food.

"Lord, bless this food and continue to keep us safe. Amen." It was the shortest blessing Brady had ever given, but the moment Eva was given a sip of her chocolate milk and a french fry, she stopped whining.

The tension eased from the room as they all dug into their meal.

No one spoke, maybe in deference to Shelby's and Eva's presence. Once they were finished, Reed said, "What we need is a satellite computer. Something we can route through a server that won't give away our location."

"Ian is working on that," Brady said between bites of his burger. "I'm heading out soon to grab it."

"What can we do in the meantime?" Shelby asked.

Aiden turned to her. "I know I asked you this before, but I need you to think back to the conversations you had with Emmitt. Did he say anything at all that seemed out of place?"

"I told you, we didn't talk about his deployments." She sighed, dragging her fingers through her hair. "I'll try, Aiden. But he's been gone for two years." She hesitated, then added, "There are times I can barely remember what he looked like."

"I know this is difficult for you." He shouldn't have been glad to hear she had trouble remembering what Emmitt looked like. No sense in thinking it might be an indication she was ready to move on. "But anything you can come up with might help. As you can see, we're pretty much shooting in the dark."

"What about the list of female soldiers?" Shelby stared at him with tired eyes. "Isn't it likely that Emmitt had an affair with one of them?"

"Yes." Then a thought hit. "Do you have female friends? Maybe other couples you liked to do things with?"

"You're joking." She gave him an exasperated look. "Emmitt wasn't home enough for us to hang out with each other, much less engage in friendships with other couples."

Eva had devoured her chicken nuggets and fries, managing to smear a liberal amount of ketchup over her face in the process. But then she irritably pushed her half-eaten food away. "I'm all done, Mommy. I wanna get down."

"Excuse me." Shelby stood and crossed to the sink. She washed Eva's face, hands, and the table before lifting Eva to the floor. The little girl rubbed her eyes. "Come with me, Eva. We'll watch a show, okay?"

Surprisingly, Eva nodded and followed Shelby down the hall to the master bedroom. He remembered seeing a television in there.

"She's right about the list of female soldiers," Heath said. "We need to crossmatch them with Tim Tobin. Maybe he's very close to one of them, close enough to come after Shelby and Eva."

"I still think he was hired by the real perp, but we can keep digging." Aiden glanced at Brady. "How soon can you pick up the satellite computer?"

"Leaving now." Brady wiped his mouth with a napkin and stood. "You're on kitchen clean-up duty."

"I'll do it," Kyleigh said with a sigh.

"I'll dry," Marc offered. When Kyleigh sent him a surprised look, he grinned. "Kari would expect no less."

"I can't wait to meet your wife." Kyleigh gathered their garbage together. "Elly's trying to coordinate something with Maddy Sinclair over the holiday."

"Yeah, we have strict orders to clear our schedules." Marc carried the few plates and cups they'd used to the sink. "Should be fun."

Aiden had nothing against Elly and Maddy's planned family reunion, but they had bigger problems facing them.

If they didn't get to the bottom of this mess, there may be one less Finnegan in attendance.

———

SHELBY WAS grateful Eva fell asleep within minutes. She eased out of the bed and tiptoed to the door. She wanted nothing more than to take a nap herself, but she knew that wasn't fair.

Aiden expected her to contribute to this investigation. And she'd racked her brain, unable to come up with anything useful.

She returned to the kitchen in time to see Aiden opening the laptop. "Wait. I thought you we needed one powered by a satellite?"

"That's for Heath to use." Aiden tapped the device. "This has only been used to search social media. I don't think it's been tracked, not the way an army-issued computer would be."

"If you say so." She dropped into the chair beside him.

Heath frowned. "I know you told me about your top suspects, but how are you weeding the others out?"

"My system isn't perfect. There were two women who I didn't find anything about, so I can't rule them out completely. I was hoping you could help vet those for us. For now, I'm just looking for anyone with a high probability of being involved with Emmitt Copeland." He pointed to the next name on the list, the one beneath Amy Golden. Shelby felt sick all over again at realizing the young woman had killed herself. "Jane Fordham is the next one I was planning to look into."

Heath nodded. "Let's do it. Maybe we'll get lucky."

"Have faith," Marc said over his shoulder. "That's better than luck."

It was awkward watching Aiden work. Especially when she was so tired it was hard to see straight. She finally stood and moved away, pacing the living room to get her blood circulating.

"There are a lot of Jane Fordhams," Heath said. "How will we figure out which one was in the service?"

"We look at all of them." Aiden's determination was admirable.

"That one," Heath said. "Her bio says she's in the reserves."

"Looks as if she hasn't posted in a while," Aiden said.

Her curiosity piqued, she returned to the table. Leaning over Aiden's shoulder, she saw another beautiful woman on the screen, only she had long auburn hair rather than blond. "How long since her last post?"

"Looks like eighteen months." Aiden sat back in his chair, his gaze zeroed in on the image. "Emmitt died two years ago. The time frame of her going dark on the platform could be significant."

"Or maybe she just decided to get off social media." She shrugged. "I don't think it's that big of a deal."

"Maybe." She could tell Aiden thought otherwise. "Let's make a note to check her out when Brady returns with the satellite computer."

"Looks like I'll be checking most of these names." Heath sighed.

"I know. But it's nice to put a face with a name," Aiden pointed out. "Even if it's only a few of them."

They got through three more names, eliminating only one of them as the woman was pictured with her soldier husband and five-year-old son, before Brady returned with the satellite computer. She found herself hoping the process would go faster now that Heath could access the army database.

The sat computer was tricky to set up, but once it was positioned close to a window, Heath was able to log in. "Where do you want me to start?"

"Amy Golden," she answered quicker than Aiden. At his surprised look, she grimaced. "Her suicide is haunting me. I need to know if she's involved."

"I've already determined she doesn't have a husband, brother, or father in the National Guard," Heath protested. "It's better if we move on to someone else."

She bit her lip, then nodded. "Okay, fine. But I'd still like to understand why she killed herself."

"We may never know," Aiden said, his gaze full of empathy. "Suicide victims often hide their depression from those around them, even their closest family members."

"Fine." She decided to let it go, telling herself there was no proof that Emmitt played a role in the young woman taking her life.

"Can you look into the personnel file of Justine Brooks?" Aiden asked. "It might help to cross her off the list."

She remembered Justine was the stunning beauty that Aiden had identified as leaving the army. The woman who she could easily imagine Emmitt sleeping with behind her back.

Heath tapped a few keys, then scanned the information. "She has one disciplinary action related to fraternizing with an officer."

"Does it say which officer?" Aiden asked.

"No, but that isn't unusual." Heath shrugged. "The

officer would receive a disciplinary action as well, and his file would not reveal her name either. Whatever happened couldn't be too serious because the officer involved would have been demoted or kicked out of the National Guard. Nothing like that is noted here."

"Would his action be noted in her personnel file?" Shelby asked. She remembered hearing Emmitt didn't have any disciplinary action in his file.

Heath considered this. "Most of the time it is noted. Especially if there is a need to protect the female soldier from retribution."

As far as Shelby was concerned, taking the time to describe what the officer had suffered without naming him seemed like splitting hairs. Then again, the army didn't always make sense. Like most government run agencies, there were many inconsistencies.

"How long ago was the disciplinary action?" Aiden asked.

"Three years ago." Heath glanced at him. "I guess Emmitt Copeland could be involved as he was alive then."

"Except for the fact that I already looked at his file, and Tom Mitchell did too. His record is clean, which is why the rumor of his having an affair was never substantiated." Heath shot her a sympathetic look. "Based on that, it's not likely he was involved with Justine Brooks."

"Unless a superior officer was covering for him," she pointed out. "Maybe even because that same officer knew my father." Another thought struck. "Maybe that was why Kevin Carter asked if there were any files at my father's home."

There was a long moment of silence as Aiden and Heath digested this. "That's a possibility," Aiden admitted. "But we can't go too far into the what-if scenarios. For now, let's look for something more obvious. I have a feeling your father may have uncovered the truth, and that's why this is blowing up now, two years after Emmitt's death."

She reluctantly nodded. At this rate, they'd never get through the list long enough to create viable suspects.

The thought was depressing.

Heath and Aiden worked for a solid twenty minutes while Brady and Marc huddled in the living room with another computer. She wasn't sure what they were working on, but she hoped it was something that would break this case wide open.

"Go back to Jane Fordham," Aiden said. "I'm curious if you can find a reason for her to have dropped off social media eighteen months ago."

More key tapping, then Heath said, "Looks like she went out on medical leave and didn't return to the National Guard."

"Wait, I thought she was still active?" Aiden scowled at the list. "Tom pulled those female soldiers who were still in the military."

"The paperwork isn't always as up to date as it should be," Heath said. "Wait a minute."

Shelby's heart thudded against her ribs. "What is it?"

Heath let out a low whistle. "Looks like she had a baby."

A baby? Emmitt's baby? Did Eva have a half brother or sister?

Bile rose in the back of her throat. She clapped her hand over her mouth and bolted from the room. Ducking into the bathroom, she slammed the door and immediately lost her lunch.

# CHAPTER TWELVE

Aiden jumped to his feet, quickly rushing after Shelby. Only to stop short when she slammed the bathroom door in his face. He winced when he heard her retching. Feeling helpless, he stood there, wishing for a way to make this easier for her.

He knew she'd assumed the baby was Emmitt's. His mind had gone there, too, despite the fact that they had no proof. It could be that Jane Fordham had been with someone else. For Shelby's sake, he silently prayed that wasn't the case.

When there was nothing but silence on the other side of the door, he called, "Shelby? Are you okay? May I come in?"

No answer.

He hesitated, unwilling to breach her privacy. Yet he wanted her to know she wasn't alone. That he was there for her no matter what.

Another long moment passed before he heard water running in the sink. Finally, the door opened. She didn't meet his gaze, but said, "I'm fine."

"I don't see how you can be fine," he murmured. Gently pushing the door open a bit farther, he drew her into his arms. "Don't torture yourself over this. We don't know anything for certain."

"I know." To his relief, she leaned against him. He drew her closer still, running his hand down her back. "It's just the possibility hadn't occurred to me until Heath mentioned she had a baby."

"Which may or may not be related to what is going on here." Heart aching, he pressed a kiss to the top of her head. "Thinking the worst isn't going to help. We need to deal with facts, not fiction."

"But what if Eva has a brother or sister out there?" Her voice was filled with anguish. "I should reach out to the child's mother. It wouldn't be fair to keep the siblings isolated from each other. They should meet and spend time together."

"Okay, hold on a minute." He loved the way she wanted to bring the kids together, but this entire line of thinking was a huge leap. "Our priority is to figure out who and why someone is trying to kill you. It's highly possible we're on the wrong track here, that Emmitt wasn't involved with this woman at all. Don't go too far off track. Let's stay focused on the immediate threat."

She nodded, her face still buried against his chest. "I know you're right. That it's not even likely that Emmitt had a child with some other woman . . . but then again, I didn't even know about his affair."

Aiden wished Emmitt was still alive so he could punch the guy for putting her through this. "Even that hasn't been proven yet. Try to put your faith in God that this will work out according to His plan."

She let out a harsh laugh. "Really? His plan? Why

would God allow me to marry a man who would betray me like this?"

"I don't know. But God always has a reason." He couldn't think of a way to reassure her this would all work out. They were still operating in the dark as far as having viable suspects was concerned. "There's a Bible verse our pastor uses frequently, from 1 Chronicles 16:11 that says, 'Seek the Lord and his strength, seek him continually.' This always helps me when I'm in stressful situations. And know that I'm here for you, Shelby. Lean on me. There's no reason for you to struggle through this alone."

"That's a nice verse. And truly, Aiden, you've been wonderful." She let out a jagged sigh, then slowly lifted her head to look up at him. "I'm sorry to fall apart like that."

"Don't apologize for being upset." He searched her damp gaze. "You've been through so much, Shelby. More than most women face in a lifetime."

"Yeah, but there are others who have it worse too." She shook her head. "I'm a teacher, some of my students come from broken homes or have parents battling cancer. There's no point in comparing one person's situation to another's. This is my reality, and I'll have to find a way to deal with it moving forward."

"Just remember you're not alone." He almost promised to be there for her even after this was over, but he hadn't made any decisions about his future yet. Not to mention, his siblings all lived in the Milwaukee area.

Yet even as he considered that, he knew it wasn't enough to keep him from Shelby. Oshkosh wasn't that far, just an hour away. Close enough to get together during the holidays.

Wait a minute, was he really planning a future with

Shelby and Eva? Talk about a stretch. He wasn't sure she'd want to see him again once they were safe.

"Thank you." Shelby brushed a chaste kiss against his cheek. "I would be lost without you." A sad smile creased her features. "I guess we should get back to the kitchen."

"Yeah." He wasn't ready to face the others, but of course, they needed to keep working, searching for a link between the gunman Tim Tobin and whoever may have hired him. He slipped his arm around her waist. "Ready?"

She nodded. Brady, Marc, Kyleigh, and Heath glanced over when they walked in. To his credit, Heath didn't ask about Shelby but went right into work mode. "The good news is that we've been able to rule out two women."

"Great. Nothing yet on a connection between Parsons and Tobin?"

Heath grimaced. "Only that Tobin was a soldier under Parsons's command. But that alone doesn't mean much. He had lots of soldiers under his care." Heath hesitated, then added, "Including Jane Fordham."

"Parsons obviously knew about Fordham's pregnancy," Brady surmised. "Or at least, he'd processed her medical leave paperwork."

"I imagine many people knew about it," Shelby said, commenting for the first time since the announcement of Fordham's having a child. "Speaking from experience, it's hard to hide morning sickness. Unless she happened to be one of the few who didn't suffer from that affliction."

"You make a good point," Marc said. "Kari was really sick during both of her pregnancies."

"Devon was too. Let's keep searching," Brady suggested, catching Aiden's gaze. His brother could read his intense desire to change the subject. "We are still a long way from having anything concrete to go on."

"It may be time to meet directly with Bill Parsons." Aiden tried not to sound as impatient as he felt.

"He's a senior officer and not obligated to talk to us," Heath pointed out.

"That doesn't mean we can't interview him." He glanced at Shelby, who still looked pale. "Maybe he'll let something slip."

"Not if he's involved," Brady said. "And at this point, he's the most likely suspect to have tracked Heath Strauss to the farmhouse." Brady's phone rang, startling the group. "Hold on, this is our boss." He rose and moved into the other room. "Donovan? What's up?"

There was a hushed silence as Brady spoke to the special agent in charge. Then he returned to the kitchen. "Tim Tobin is still in surgery. At this point, it looks as if he'll make it."

"That's a relief," Reed said.

"Any idea how long it will be until we can talk to him?" Aiden asked. "We'd be much further along if he could tell us who hired him."

"Not yet, but Donovan has asked the local police to have an officer stationed outside his room." Brady shrugged. "Hopefully once he wakes up, he'll tell us what we want to know."

Aiden knew that could easily take another twenty-four hours. "I'm glad there's a cop sitting on him."

"Me too." Brady shrugged. "In the meantime, we keep digging.

"I thought Donovan was getting us a list of soldiers who were discharged dishonorably by Shelby's father?" Being under fire had caused him to lose track of the threads they still had left to investigate.

"I forgot about that. I'll check with Donovan." Brady turned away to make the call.

"I feel like we're getting nowhere fast," Shelby said with a sigh.

"Well, I just crossed another woman off the list," Heath announced. "But here's another possibility, Suzanne Potter."

"What about her?" Aiden asked.

"She has a post about how the army takes advantage of women, believing male counterparts over the women." Heath grimaced. "I'm checking her personnel record now."

Thrilled with the possibility of another lead, Aiden leaned closer to read the screen. Then he sighed. "I don't see anything in her file."

"Yeah, it's clean." Heath looked disappointed too. "I'll keep her on the list of possible suspects, though, just in case."

"I'm disappointed there are so many women who aren't happy being in the service," Kyleigh said with a frown. "I'd think we'd be further along on the path to equal rights by now."

"I hear you." Heath glanced at her. "Like every other profession, it's the small handful of morons who ruin it for the rest."

"You've got that right," Aiden agreed. "I have not had much trouble with my team. And I would hope if there was something going on, it would be reported up the chain of command."

"Some women feel like that only hurts their chances of getting ahead," Kyleigh said. "I've been grateful to have awesome superiors. But I also don't complain about every little thing that gets said either. I ignore some of the crap, unless it's really bad."

Aiden knew she was insinuating that the handful of female soldiers he'd worked with may be doing the same thing.

"Okay, Donovan has the list," Brady announced. He worked his phone. "I'm sending that to you, Heath. We need to start crossmatching those names with our possible suspects."

"Got it," Heath said, then glanced up. "No surprise that Tim Tobin is on the list."

"My father discharged him?" Shelby asked in surprise. "Maybe that's the answer. Tim was angry and upset with my father, so he's taking his anger out on me."

"Maybe," Aiden said. He wanted more than anything for the danger to be over. "We won't know for sure until we can talk to him."

Shelby nodded. "I get that, but looking for a woman Emmitt had an affair with could be nothing but a distraction."

Aiden glanced at Heath, who shrugged. His gut was telling him that this was more personal than a dishonorable discharge.

But then again, they hadn't stumbled across anything resembling a smoking gun yet either.

"Mommy?" Eva's voice called out from the bedroom.

Shelby stood and hurried down the hall. "I'm here, Eva. It's okay." Her voice faded as she entered the bedroom.

There was a brief silence as they looked at each other.

"Unfortunately, I don't think it's that simple." Brady's voice was low so it wouldn't carry down the hall.

"Me either," Marc added.

"I wish it was, but I doubt it," Aiden said.

Heath and Kyleigh nodded. "So we keep working," Kyleigh said.

"Yeah." He scrubbed his face with his hands. Somehow, he had a bad feeling that Tim Tobin would be replaced by someone else.

They needed to figure out who was pulling the strings before they were found again.

---

EVA RUBBED her eyes with her fists, then peered up at Shelby as if perturbed. "I don't wanna nap."

"That's fine." She hid a smile at how her daughter didn't seem to realize she'd already taken one. "Let's go to the bathroom, then you can play."

"Okay." Eva scrambled off the bed. Shelby tried not to imagine another little girl or boy who had also lost their father. Her stomach clenched as her previous nausea returned, so she did her best to push that thought out of her mind.

The possibility of Emmitt having fathered another child was a problem for a different day. Making herself sick wasn't going to help. She needed to stay strong for Eva's sake.

Being held by Aiden had helped her feel better. She'd appreciated the Bible verse he'd told her and knew it was time to lean on prayer.

There had to be a reason for this turmoil. Maybe it was even God's intent for her to know about Emmitt's infidelity. In some ways, it eased the guilt she had over not missing him as much as she'd thought she should.

Back in those early days, she blamed it on the fact that he was often deployed for long periods of time. That she'd gotten used to functioning on her own, without him.

But maybe it was more than that. Deep down, she'd

caught herself wondering if they were well suited. Each time he'd come home from a deployment, it seemed as if they'd needed to get to know each other again. Almost like they were strangers. And now she knew they were. She'd never have married Emmitt if she'd suspected he was the type to cheat.

Whatever. There was no reason to dwell on feelings she may or may not have had for Emmitt. He was gone. As Aiden had mentioned, Eva's safety was her primary concern.

Too bad she was losing all hope they'd ever figure out who was behind these attempts to kill her.

She took a moment to wash up in the bathroom after helping Eva. When they emerged, Aiden was there, hovering in the doorway.

"Hi." He looked so incredibly handsome standing there. "Just wanted to check on you."

"We're fine." She must have looked really bad earlier to warrant this level of concern. She managed a smile. "Eva wants to play."

"Sound good." Aiden grinned. "Me and my sisters used to make a fort in the living room."

"A fort?" Eva looked at him curiously. "What's that?"

"I'll show you." Aiden held out his hand, and Eva skipped over to take it. Her heart did a little flip in her chest at how Aiden made a point of connecting with her daughter.

He'd be an amazing father.

Aiden took the sofa cushions off and draped a blanket over them. Eva crawled underneath with her farm animals and her dolly.

Satisfied Eva would be preoccupied for a while, she followed Aiden back into the kitchen. On the counter, she noticed there was a container of cold fries. They tasted horrible, but she nibbled on them anyway.

Aiden must have noticed because he reached into the bag to pull out a spare burger. He tossed it in the microwave, then handed it to her.

"Thank you." She was touched at how in tune he was to her needs.

"Okay, here's something." Heath looked up from the screen. "I found another young woman who passed away last year."

The piece of burger lodged in her throat. She swallowed hard. "Another suicide?"

"I'm still looking. Her name was Kimberly Mason." Heath held her gaze for a moment as if asking if that name rang a bell.

She was about to say no but paused. "There was a Kim who came to Emmitt's funeral. I can't remember her last name."

"Here's a picture." Heath turned the computer screen toward her. Kim was pretty, but not in a stunningly beautiful way.

"There were a lot of soldiers there, and most were in uniform." She slowly shook her head. "I can't say for sure. I only remember the name Kim because Emmitt wanted to name Eva Kimmy."

"How did you come up with Eva?" Aiden asked. He seemed genuinely interested. "Did you flip a coin?"

"No." She shrugged. "I liked Eva better, and since Emmitt wasn't there throughout the labor and delivery, I told him I had already named our baby Eva and that was that. He was smart enough not to argue."

"Good for you," Kyleigh said. "I love the name Eva. It's beautiful."

"Thanks." She turned back to Heath. "Is there a way to find out more about how Kimberly died?"

"I've put in a request to see the ME's report." Heath sighed. "Hopefully, they'll get back to me."

A phone rang, and she noticed Brady jumped to his feet. "Donovan? Please tell me you have something."

Humbling to realize how hard they were all working on her behalf. Brady wasn't on the phone for long. He returned less than a minute later. "Bill Parsons is on his way to the FBI office building to meet with Donovan, and he's demanding to meet with you, Aiden, too. ASAP."

Aiden jumped up. "That works for me. How soon can we go?"

Brady grinned. "I told Donovan you and Shelby would jump at the chance to be there. He agreed to have both of you come in."

"What about Eva?" Shelby glanced at Aiden, then back to Brady. "Will your boss be okay if she comes with us?"

"Of course. That's not a problem." Brady turned to Marc. "I was hoping you would stay here with Heath Strauss."

"You don't trust me?" Heath asked.

"Yes, but you have our satellite computer, and we had to sign off in blood that we'd return it in one piece," Brady joked. "Seriously, after the way Mitchell was shot and killed, it's better if you're not here alone. Marc can stay and keep watch."

"What about us?" Kyleigh asked, gesturing to Reed. "What can we do?"

"I'm hoping you'll escort us to the FBI office building." Brady's smile faded. "From this point on, we don't go anywhere without backup."

"I agree," Aiden said somberly. He stood and added, "Let's hit the road. Maybe we can beat Parsons there."

Eva, of course, wasn't thrilled at taking yet another car ride, but Shelby managed to wrestle the little girl into her coat, hat, and mittens. She then made sure to take Eva's dolly and farm animals along for the ride.

"Brady, why don't you take a vehicle and leave first?" Aiden suggested as they prepared to go outside. "Kyleigh and Reed can follow behind. The caravan approach has been working so far. I'd rather not mess with success."

"No problem." Brady opened the door, then stepped across the threshold. He took a moment to scan the area, then gestured for them to move forward. "It's clear."

Accustomed to the routine by now, Shelby picked up Eva and followed him. Aiden stayed right behind her as they reached the SUVs parked in the driveway. He continued hovering the entire time it took to buckle the three-year-old in the car. Then he opened her door for her before sliding in behind the wheel.

"How long will it take to get to the FBI office?" she asked, glancing at Aiden.

"Fifteen to twenty minutes." He shrugged. "The roads are nicely cleared now, and the sun is out, so weather shouldn't be a factor."

"Yeah." She didn't mention how big the city seemed compared to where her small suburban home was located. On snowy days, she could walk to school if the district hadn't canceled classes.

"Isn't today Saturday?" She frowned. "I'm surprised Brady's boss would schedule a meeting with Sergeant Major Bill Parsons over the weekend."

"These are not normal circumstances." Aiden grimaced.

"Especially not with these escalated attacks. Personally, I'm glad the FBI is taking this seriously."

She nodded, offering a crooked smile. "It's not looking good for me to be in the classroom on Monday."

"Not unless Parsons gives us a clue as to what's going on." He took her hand in his. "Hopefully, this will be over soon. But if your principal needs advance notice to find a substitute teacher, you should probably let them know now that you won't be there."

"I don't have his number memorized." She frowned. "I can get the secretary's number off the website when we get back to the safe house."

"Sounds good." Aiden frowned. "Looks like the road is closed."

Since she wasn't familiar with the city, she didn't have anything to add.

Aiden turned, following Brady as he took the detour. They drove in silence for several minutes. Aiden let out a low groan when Brady crossed a railroad track seconds before the red lights came on and two gates lowered to block traffic from both sides of the road.

"Rotten timing." Aiden scowled at the cargo train that began rolling past. "I hope this isn't a long one."

"They always are when in a hurry," she teased.

"At least Kyleigh and Reed are behind us." He glanced at the rearview mirror. "Brady will likely pull off and wait too."

She wasn't worried. The train was noisy, and Eva began counting the cars as they went past. Unfortunately, she kept getting them out of order.

"Two, five, one, ten," Eva used her cow to point to the window. "I can't count that many."

"It's okay." The words were barely out of her mouth when she heard a crack of thunder.

"Down! Get down!" Aiden pushed her head down and twisted in his seat.

Not thunder—gunfire! The SUV tilted to the driver's side as another loud crack could be heard over the rumbling of the train.

Had one of their tires been hit? *Eva!* What if the next bullet pierced the rear window and killed her daughter?

She pushed Aiden's hand away and unlatched her seatbelt. She began to crawl through the opening between the front seats when suddenly she saw a flash of movement.

"Stay here," Aiden shouted.

Seconds later Kyleigh and Reed were there, each opening a door on the passenger side of the car. Kyleigh unbuckled Eva, picking up the little girl and cradling her close, while Reed helped her out of the car.

"This way," Reed shouted.

Aiden came around to join them. As always, he positioned himself so that he was behind her. She followed Reed and Kyleigh toward a driveway. She belatedly realized there was a parking lot leading to an apartment complex not far from the train tracks. Without hesitation, the four of them raced that way, seeking shelter behind the three-story brick building.

"Brady! We're under fire," Aiden shouted as they ran. "We need you here ASAP!"

Her thoughts whirled as Reed led the way inside the lobby of the apartment building. It wasn't large, but to the right there was a common area that appeared to be open and not in use.

"Go inside," Reed directed curtly. "I'll stay here with Aiden."

Shelby nodded, following Kyleigh and Eva into the room. Kyleigh went to the farthest corner, pulled a chair around, and used it as a shield.

"Sit here with Eva on your lap." Kyleigh gently pushed the little girl into her arms. "I'll stand guard here; the guys will watch the door."

She nodded, cuddling her daughter close. But the mantra that ran through her mind was that Sergeant Major Bill Parsons had to have set this up.

There was no one else who'd known they were on their way to the FBI building.

# CHAPTER THIRTEEN

"Looks like the rear tire was hit." Aiden didn't want to admit the ambush had caught him off guard, but it had.

He should have been prepared for this.

He and Reed stood guard on either side of the glass doors leading into the small lobby of the apartment building. For being what appeared to be a nice place, there wasn't much security. Anyone could walk inside. Granted, the doors were probably locked at night, but that wasn't much help in keeping riffraff out.

"I see it." Reed called Brady, putting the call on speaker. "Gunfire while waiting on train, the Jeep SUV incapacitated, the other is okay. Everyone is safe, but we need an extraction plan."

If Aiden didn't know better, he'd assume Reed had also been in the army.

"Stay put. I'm on my way," Brady said.

Reed disconnected from the phone. "The shooter was on the driver's side of the vehicle."

Aiden glanced at his soon-to-be brother-in-law. "What did you see?"

"Nothing really, but when the tire blew, I glanced in that direction. There was some movement within the trees, but nothing I can say with certainty resembling a shooter hiding in wait."

"I don't understand why the tire was hit." Aiden swept his gaze over the area outside the apartment doorway. "From that vantage point, the shooter could have taken me out. That way Shelby and Eva would be easy pickings."

"I agree, the strategy doesn't make sense. Even if the shooter didn't realize you had us behind you, why not set up on the passenger side of the road?"

"Why would the shooter set up here at all?" Aiden frowned. "Bill Parsons has to be involved. No one else from the army knew about us heading to the FBI office."

"I agree." Reed also kept his gaze trained out the window, searching for a sign of the shooter.

"What is going on here?"

Aiden turned to see a plump woman roughly in her fifties standing behind them. Her eyes popped when she saw the weapon in his hand.

"Gun!" she shrieked, and held her hands up, taking several steps backward. "Why are you here with guns?"

"There was a shooter outside, ma'am," Aiden said calmly. "I'm with the National Guard, and Reed Carmichael is with the Milwaukee Police Department. You're safe as long as you stay inside."

"You don't look like police! You're not wearing uniforms!" This woman was bordering on hysteria, her head shifting from side to side as if looking for an escape route. "I'm calling them right now!"

"That's fine, ma'am." Aiden had to assume some of the other witnesses who were sitting in their cars waiting for the train had already done that too. Besides, it didn't matter if the police were notified. They wouldn't be there long. The minute Brady arrived they'd hit the road.

They needed to get to the FBI office as soon as possible. Especially after this latest shooting. Then a thought struck him. What if Bill Parsons didn't bother to show for the meeting with Donovan? This could be nothing than a plan to get them out of the safe house.

A plan that had worked.

Ignoring the woman speaking urgently on the phone with the 911 dispatcher, Aiden continued watching the road. When Brady's SUV pulled up, he almost sighed in relief.

"Brady's here." He glanced over to where Kyleigh stood in front of Shelby and Eva. The little girl was still playing with her farm animals, clueless as to the danger they were in.

He was glad for that because dealing with a hysterical child along with the woman screeching into the phone behind him would be a lot.

"Okay, Shelby," Kyleigh said. "I want you and Eva to stay close. I'll get you safely into Brady's SUV."

Aiden appreciated his sister stepping up to help. He nodded at Reed, and the two of them stepped through the glass door of the apartment first, each fanning out a bit to scour the area. Reassured, he quickly moved toward the SUV. He noticed the train had passed, and traffic was moving along the road. Well, sort of. The cars had to swing around Reed's car, which was sitting behind the disabled Jeep.

He opened the back passenger door for Shelby.

"Wait!" She stopped abruptly. "I need the car seat for Eva!"

Aiden tamped down a flash of frustration. Obviously, he wanted Eva to be safe, and that meant getting far away from here.

"I'll get it." Reed holstered his weapon, then jogged over to where the disabled car sat. He made quick work of removing the car seat, then brought it over.

"Thanks." Shelby shot Reed a grateful look as Aiden took the car seat and buckled it in. "I'm glad you brought her dolly too. Thank goodness she had the other farm animals in her hands."

"Nooo," Eva wailed. "I don't wanna ride in the car!"

Shelby's features were strained as she fought to get her toddler into the car seat. When Eva tried to hit her mother with the cow, Shelby took it from her hands. "No hitting," she said sharply. "Settle down. We need to go. We'll sing songs on the way, okay?"

Being on the run with a three-year-old wasn't easy. Even with the few toys they'd managed to hang on to for her. After what seemed like forever, Eva was securely fastened in her car seat. Shelby dropped into the seat next to her.

"Get up front," Reed said. "Kyleigh and I will follow, same formation as before."

He didn't waste time arguing. He ran around to jump in beside Brady. Reed and Kyleigh ran out to get into their SUV. Reed backed it up, then gestured for Brady to pull out.

The wail of police sirens could be heard as they drove away. Aiden imagined the plump woman would fill them in on the two gunmen who'd barged into the apartment building. He scrubbed his hands over his face for a moment, then shoved that concern aside.

"Fill me in," Brady said.

"There's not much to tell. The shooter was on the driver's side of the road. Took out our tire. Kyleigh and Reed came to get Shelby and Eva out of harm's way. We took shelter in the apartment building located on the passenger side of the road." Aiden shrugged. "Truthfully, it doesn't make sense. I guess it's possible the shooter didn't want to take me out, but removing innocent men hasn't stopped him before now."

"Maybe the goal was abduction," Brady said thoughtfully. It hadn't been that long ago that Caleb had been taken from his bed by a guy looking for a hefty ransom.

"If that is the case, why do that now?" He glanced back to see Shelby playing with Eva to keep the little girl occupied. "So far these have been shooting attempts. Why the change in MO?"

"I don't know," Brady admitted.

"We were sitting ducks out there." He kept his voice low, unwilling to upset Shelby. Not that she wasn't smart enough to figure things out on her own. "Any shooter within the army could have eliminated all of us with three well-placed shots."

"We'll figure this out," Brady said in a reassuring tone. "I put a call in to Donovan but haven't heard back."

"I wouldn't be surprised if Parsons was a no-show," Aiden said.

"He's the one behind these attacks, isn't he?" Shelby asked.

He turned to look at her. "That was my first thought. Although it could be that someone pretending to be Parsons made the call to Donovan to set up the meeting, then took the time to ambush us. Hard to say for sure."

"How did the shooter know we'd take that route?" Shelby frowned. "There were other ways to get to the FBI office building."

"We took that route because the main road was closed." He winced at how easily they'd fallen into that trap. Anyone could put up roadblock signs.

"We still could have taken the interstate, though," she protested.

"Yeah, but maybe the shooter anticipated we wouldn't, not after the way Mitchell was shot and killed."

"I don't like this," Shelby whispered.

"Try not to worry." Brady glanced up at the rearview mirror. "We'll know more once we get to the office."

"I hope so," Aiden said. "But if Parsons doesn't show, there won't be anything more we can do there."

"Considering how this latest attack went down, I'll convince Donovan to go farther up the chain of command within the army and also within the bureau." Brady's expression was grim. "No way this was a coincidence."

"That would be great." Aiden took heart in knowing more upper brass would be involved. As much as he appreciated and valued his family, they couldn't outrun this gunman forever. They needed answers.

"I don't think my father got along with Bill Parsons," Shelby said.

That surprised him. He twisted in his seat to look at her. "What makes you say that?"

She shrugged. "He didn't say that in so many words, but I know he and Parsons climbed the ranks together. I think they served together at some point."

"Okay, but what specifically did your father say about him?" he pressed.

She frowned, her gaze turning thoughtful. "I can't remember the exact words. But I know he came home one day and said something like, 'Any idiot can be promoted, look at how far Bill has come' or something like that. I just got the impression he wasn't impressed with the guy."

That was a far cry from attempting to murder a colleague's daughter and granddaughter, but there was likely more to the relationship between the two men.

Something he planned to ask the guy point-blank if Parsons really did show up to meet with Donovan.

Thankfully, the trip to the FBI offices located in Ravenswood was uneventful. Yet as Brady pulled into the parking lot, with Kyleigh and Reed right behind them, he turned to Shelby.

"You and Eva stay put until we're ready."

She nodded, then began to gather the little girl's toys. "We're getting out of the car, Eva."

"I have'ta go to the bafroom."

Of course, she did. He should have anticipated that. It seemed little kids had bladders the size of a peanut. At least they were heading into a secure location.

"Soon," he promised Eva. He took a moment to secure his weapon in the glove box, knowing the feds wouldn't allow him to keep the gun. Then he pushed open his car door and slid out as Brady did the same.

Kyleigh and Reed quickly joined them, also without their sidearms, he noted. The four of them crowded around the vehicle until Brady called his IT colleague to make sure there was nothing suspicious in the area around the building. After a shooting in the parking lot just a few weeks ago, Aiden knew the feds had added even more security cameras.

"Okay, let's go." Brady gave him a nod.

He opened the door to reach Eva while Shelby slid out on the other side. Seconds later, they were safely inside the nondescript brown-brick federal office building.

For the first time since leaving the safe house, Aiden felt as if they were out of the line of fire. Brady hustled them into the building, putting their names on a list and then gesturing toward the bathrooms. Shelby gratefully took Eva into the women's room.

Once they were cleared and provided visitor badges, Brady opened the door to a large conference room. "Wait here."

He nodded, glancing to where Shelby was taking Eva's winter coat off. He didn't have the heart to tell her they likely wouldn't be here that long.

Long minutes passed. Reed and Kyleigh glanced around curiously. He was more interested in speaking with Sergeant Major Parsons.

Finally, the door to the conference room opened. A tall man dressed in a suit entered first, followed by a short man wearing a full-dress military uniform. Presumably Parsons. Lastly, Brady stepped inside.

Parsons drilled Aiden with a narrow gaze, and he belatedly saluted his senior officer. Parsons returned the salute, but the banked anger in the guy's gaze didn't lessen. "Staff Sergeant Finnegan?"

"Yes, sir." Aiden wasn't in uniform, having changed days ago after the funeral.

"You're under arrest." Parsons turned toward Donovan. "Thanks for arranging this meeting. I'll take it from here."

"Under arrest? For what?" Aiden didn't look away from Parsons. The guy was guilty of trying to kill Shelby and Eva, although obviously not doing the deed himself.

"The murder of Emmitt Copeland."

His jaw dropped. Wow. He hadn't seen that one coming.

---

AIDEN ARRESTED? What was going on? Shelby didn't believe Aiden was guilty of anything, but Parsons was intimidating in his uniform and dark scowl. She instinctively moved closer to Reed and Kyleigh, unsure of what to expect.

"Hold on." The man dressed in a suit and tie that she presumed was Special Agent in Charge Donovan held up a hand, stepping forward to place himself between Aiden and Parsons. "You never said anything about arresting anyone."

"I don't have to tell you anything," Parsons said in a snide tone. "This is army business. I'm Finnegan's superior officer. I absolutely have the ability to arrest him."

"Technically, you need the military police to do that," Aiden said. "Besides, the charge is bogus. I didn't kill Emmitt Copeland."

"That's for a jury to decide." Parsons didn't look as if he cared one way or the other. "I can have two military police officers here in less than five minutes."

Shelby noticed the flash of concern between Brady and Kyleigh. Her heart sank. Was this how Parsons planned to do this? Set up a fake arrest to get Aiden out of the way, leaving her vulnerable to another attack?

A shiver ran down her spine. Before she could voice her concern, Kyleigh sent her a reassuring smile. She took a deep breath and let it out slowly. She didn't want Aiden to be arrested, but she knew that if that did happen, the Finnegans wouldn't abandon her and Eva. And that meant a lot to her. Family loyalty she didn't deserve.

"Be careful, Parsons. I'm pretty sure I'll be able to convince the MPs to arrest you," Aiden said with a pointed look. "We have your second shooter in custody. Sloppy work on your part. Your guy missed again."

Shelby did her best not to look surprised by his statement.

"I don't know what you're talking about," Parsons looked down his nose at Aiden, no easy task since the older man was five inches shorter. "Deflecting blame for your deeds onto me isn't going to work."

"Actually, I'm with the staff sergeant on this one." Donovan turned and grabbed one of Parsons's wrists. Brady stepped up to grab the other. "The fact that there was a shooter stationed along the route Aiden and Agent Brady Finnegan took to come here deserves further investigation. You're in federal custody now, Parsons."

The man's face turned beet red to the point Shelby feared he'd suffer a heart attack, similar to the massive coronary that killed her father. "You can't do this," Parsons sputtered.

"Mommy, why are they yelling?" Eva asked.

"Shh." She bent to pick Eva up, holding her close. "They're having a disagreement, that's all."

The scene continued to unfold without anyone paying attention to her daughter.

"See, you're here on my turf, so yeah, I can." Donovan didn't smirk as he slapped cuffs around the sergeant major's wrists. "You can stay here with us while we wait for our respective superior officers to work this out."

"What shooter? Remove these cuffs right now! I didn't kill anyone, Finnegan did!" Parsons looked flummoxed by being handcuffed. "I'll have your job for this, Donovan!

You'll never work for the federal government again, you hear me?"

"I could say the same for you, Parsons." Donovan didn't look concerned. He pushed the bound man toward the closest chair. "Sit down and tell us why you've arranged for a shooter to ambush Aiden Finnegan, Ms. Copeland, and her daughter."

"I did no such thing!" The senior officer really looked as if his head might combust, just like one of those head-exploding emojis. Shelby was grateful for having Reed and Kyleigh beside her. She wouldn't put anything past Parsons who appeared to be a desperate man.

"As soon as Tim Tobin is awake enough to be interviewed, he'll corroborate the shooter's story," Aiden said calmly. "The gig is up, Parsons. You may as well tell us everything."

"You're insane, Finnegan. You're the one who should be in cuffs, not me." Parsons appeared to pull himself together, as if sensing he was only hurting himself by losing control. "I have evidence of your culpability. We'll see whose evidence is believable when presented at a court-martial."

There was a long silence as Aiden digested this. Finally, he asked, "Who provided the evidence against me?"

Parsons sneered. "I don't have to tell you anything."

"You do if you plan on getting out of here without being tossed in a federal prison," Donovan said.

"On what charges?" Parsons asked.

Donovan leaned close. "You arranged to meet with me here, requesting Staff Sergeant Finnegan to be in attendance. Along the route to the meeting, a shooter tried to take him out of the picture. The only people who knew about the meeting are here in this room." The SAC spread his arms wide, encompassing the small group. "Care to explain that?"

For the first time, a flicker of unease crossed the officer's features. "You think I set him up? Is that what this is about?"

"I told you we have the shooter in custody," Aiden said. "He pointed the finger directly at you."

"Impossible," Parsons said sharply. "I have no reason to want you or anyone else dead. But I did plan to bring you back with me, that much is true."

Shelby swallowed hard. Was it possible Parsons was telling the truth? Had they gotten this all wrong? There was no shooter to provide evidence against the guy. Not until Tim Tobin was able to be interviewed about who had hired him.

"The fastest way to get to the bottom of this is for you to tell us who came up with evidence implicating Aiden Finnegan in Copeland's death," Brady said.

Parsons remained stubbornly silent.

"Tom Mitchell personally told me that he declared Copeland's death an accident. That there was absolutely no evidence he'd been shot on purpose." Aiden stepped closer, looking down at Parsons who was seated in a chair. "He also told me there was a rumor about Copeland having an extra-marital affair. No one would substantiate that rumor, though, so he closed the case. Then he was shot and killed."

Parsons's expression remained stoic. "I'm fully aware of what happened. I assigned an investigator to look into Mitchell's death. And maybe it is related to the Copeland investigation; then again, maybe it's not. All I know is that new evidence has come to light implicating you, Finnegan. And that changes everything." The older man narrowed his gaze. "You should know as well as anyone that there is no statute of limitations on murder."

"Yes, and that's something you should be aware of too," Aiden shot back. "Murder for hire carries the same sentence as first-degree murder. Life in Leavenworth without the possibility of parole."

The intensity of the glare leveled between the two men might have been funny if the situation wasn't so dire. Shelby wasn't afraid Aiden would be arrested now, but if Parsons was right about the evidence? She swallowed hard. What if he was taken away later?

She couldn't bear the thought of not seeing him again. Oh, the evidence would get straightened out eventually, but that could take time.

How had she gotten so attached to him so quickly? She didn't want to be in a relationship with another soldier. Once was more than enough. Yet there was no denying how handsome he was. How determined he'd been to keep her and Eva safe. Risking his own life countless times in the process.

But there was more to it than good old-fashioned physical attraction. It was everything about him. His kindness toward Eva. His strength, courage, and never-ending support throughout every step of this nightmare.

She loved him.

The realization hit hard. No, that wasn't possible.

Was it?

Eva wiggled in her arms, tired of being held.

Still reeling, she bent and lowered her daughter to the floor. Thankfully, Eva crawled back under the table to begin playing with her farm animals again.

"This is ridiculous," Parsons snapped. "If I'm really

under arrest, then I demand a lawyer." He glared at Aiden. "You'll want to get one too."

"There's no need for a lawyer if you cooperate with us in getting to the bottom of the shooting incident," Donovan said. "If you didn't hire someone to kill Ms. Copeland, then who did? Who did you talk to? Who else knew you were coming here to meet with me?"

Parsons was silent for a long moment. Shelby willed him to talk, to give them something to go on. Despite her earlier conviction in thinking Parsons had set them up, she was starting to believe the guy hadn't done it. That he'd been played for a fool by the real culprit.

It wasn't a stretch. Parsons clearly believed Aiden was responsible for her husband's death.

"I don't like being forced into providing information on an investigation," Parsons finally said. "But since you are coercing me, I'll tell you that Sergeant Oliver Kennedy came forward as the witness to you shooting Copeland." Parsons's gaze swung to her. "Apparently, Finnegan wanted Copeland's wife."

"That's not true!" Shelby shouted. "I barely knew Aiden two years ago."

"Men can turn into idiots when it comes to women," Parsons said.

"Kennedy," Brady repeated. "Isn't he the guy we discovered had a sexual harassment complaint filed against him? What was the female officer's name? Justine Brooks?"

"Yes, that's correct." Aiden's expression turned thoughtful. "I didn't believe Kennedy was involved in the shooting because he was one of the pallbearers at Sergeant Major Savage's funeral. He actually found the bullet that struck the ground inches in front of the spot Shelby and Eva were standing."

"He saw you," Parsons insisted. "And signed an affidavit to that effect."

"He's wrong." Aiden's eyes glittered with anger. "But I appreciate you giving us his name. I'm sure he's involved in this."

From the way the other Finnegans exchanged knowing looks, she knew they felt the same way. Was this the key they needed to put an end to this horrific danger?

She silently prayed that it was.

# CHAPTER FOURTEEN

Oliver Kennedy signed an affidavit claiming he'd killed Copeland. The news was shocking, but in a way, it made sense. Aiden felt certain the sergeant had done the deed himself and was placing the blame on his shoulders.

He turned to Brady. "Get in touch with Strauss. We need intel on Kennedy. There must be someone he's close to that was hurt by Emmitt Copeland. We figure that out, we find the link we need to get him arrested."

"On it." Brady stepped away, lifting his cell phone to his ear.

"The only one who is going to be arrested is you, Finnegan," Parsons barked. Aiden eyed the superior officer. He had to give the guy credit for attempting to maintain control despite being cuffed. There was no sign of Parsons's weapon. He was sure the feds refused to let the officer bring it inside.

He silently prayed for patience and wisdom as he stepped closer to Parsons. "Sir, take a moment to think this through. Why would I be risking my life and that of my family to protect Shelby and Eva Copeland if I had anything to do with killing her husband? Can't you see that the same person who killed Emmitt has now come after them? And why would Kennedy come forward after all this time, if not to frame me for something he did?"

It seemed as if his words finally sunk into the sergeant major's arrogant brain. "He claimed you paid him to keep silent but that he couldn't take living a lie."

"Trust me, you won't find any financial transactions between me and Kennedy. But putting that falsehood aside, the bigger issue is the danger stalking Shelby and Eva. There's a reason someone has targeted them."

"Uncuff me," Parsons demanded.

Donovan arched a brow. "First tell us who you talked to about this meeting. Was it Kennedy? Or someone else?"

"Kennedy and his pal, Sergeant Victor Morrison," Parsons reluctantly admitted.

"Vic?" Aiden frowned. "He was there when Kennedy signed the affidavit about how I killed Copeland?"

"No, Kennedy came to me alone on that score," Parsons said. "He came to me two days ago, and I had to discuss my next steps with my superior."

"When did you talk to Kennedy and Morrison?" Aiden pressed.

"Late yesterday. I asked Kennedy to meet with me, and he was with Morrison. I didn't go into detail, only mentioned that I was going to meet you here at the FBI offices to have you arrested."

He nodded, taking that information into consideration. It was possible Morrison was involved, either as a shooter or in some other way, but it was Kennedy who'd come forward with the story of how Aiden had paid him to remain silent about his involvement in Emmitt Copeland's death.

Glancing at Shelby, he was grateful to note she was

staring daggers at Parsons. He knew she didn't believe he was involved in her husband's death.

No, his money was on Kennedy. Only now they had to prove it.

Donovan stepped forward and removed the cuffs from Parsons's wrists. "You're free to go, but I would ask you not to talk to anyone about this, including Kennedy and Morrison. Also know you will not be taking Staff Sergeant Finnegan with you. We plan to keep your weapon, too, until we have this misunderstanding worked out."

Parsons looked as if he might argue, then he gave a curt nod. "I will wait to see what we learn from the investigation into Mitchell's death before taking further action." His senior officer pinned him with a narrow look. "Don't leave the state, Finnegan. I'm not convinced you're innocent in this."

*Ditto*, Aiden thought while trying not to roll his eyes. This act was nothing more than Parsons attempting to save face, pretending there was the possibility that he was right while Aiden and the rest of them were wrong.

Fat chance. But he hadn't gotten this far in the army without knowing when to speak up and when to shut up.

"Yes, sir." He snapped a salute.

Parsons did the same, then turned away. When he reached the conference room door, he shot back over his shoulder, "I expect to be updated on your progress, Finnegan. And that goes for Strauss too. I'd like a report by the end of the day."

Aiden didn't bother to respond because that wasn't going to happen. At least, not until they had hard-core facts to back up their suspicions.

The room fell silent after Parsons left.

"Well, that was interesting," Shelby said on a sigh.

"Yeah, but at least we have a lead." Aiden glanced at Brady. "What do you think? Is it time to head back to the safe house?"

Brady shrugged and turned to Donovan. "What do you think?"

"I think you should head back. I think it will take time for me to get more information from the guy higher up the chain of command over Parsons." Donovan offered a rare smile. "I'm looking forward to rattling the army's cage over this. In the meantime, this Oliver Kennedy sounds like a promising suspect. I'm sure your investigator can get more information on the guy than I can."

"Yeah, that's fine." Brady grimaced. "I'm sorry for putting you in the hot seat with the army, boss."

Donovan waved that away. "Don't worry. The good news is that we both work for the federal government. My boss will argue with his boss, and it will all go nowhere fast."

*Typical government*, Aiden thought. Then again, the snail's pace could work to their advantage. Hopefully, they'd have this wrapped up before the two branches of the government could lob bricks at each other. "Then we'll head back to the safe house."

Eva peeked out from beneath the conference table. "Can we go swimming?"

Where had that come from? He glanced helplessly at Shelby who sighed and shrugged. Kids. Who knew how their tiny minds worked?

"Not today, but soon," Aiden said. He planned to keep that promise. Once the danger was over and the army had Oliver Kennedy in jail, he could book another hotel room just so that Eva could go swimming. The little girl deserved at least that much.

"Not soon, *now!*" she insisted. It was all Aiden could do not to smile.

"Don't argue, Eva," Shelby warned in a stern voice. He imagined she used that same tone to keep peace in her fourth-grade classroom. "Gather up your farm animals and your dolly, okay?"

Eva pouted for a moment, then crawled back under the table. He could hear her talking to her animals, saying her mean mommy was making them go away. Glancing at Shelby, he was surprised to see she wasn't upset by the comments.

"Better she plays out her anger with her toys than lashing out at people," Shelby said by way of explanation. "At least, that's what the child psychologist said after Emmitt's death."

He hadn't known she'd taken Eva to counseling, although he could understand why. Even if the little girl didn't really understand, Shelby had probably needed emotional support herself.

And that thought brought him right back to their current situation. One in which Emmitt's buddy Oliver Kennedy had likely set up this plot to kill Shelby and her daughter.

He needed to understand the guy's motive. If Kennedy had killed Emmitt, then why come back to eliminate Shelby? What harm could Emmitt's widow do after two years?

There was key information missing here, and he hoped and prayed Heath Strauss would be able to find it.

"We'll use the same caravan approach to getting back to the safe house," Reed said, breaking into his thoughts. "Although we're going to find another route to take, one that doesn't include driving over train tracks."

"Speaking of that, I should have called to get the Jeep towed," Aiden said with a grimace.

"I took care of it," Reed assured him. "I spoke to the officers on scene too. They're perturbed we left but didn't complain too much when I informed them we were at the FBI office."

"Okay, thanks." He owed his family big time. "What would I do without you, Clark?"

Reed chuckled at his using the nickname. Last month, when Reed was hiding out with his twin, Alanna, they'd started calling him Superman, which had gotten shortened to Clark, as in Clark Kent. Thankfully, Reed hadn't seemed to mind. Maybe because that moniker was slightly better than how they called Bax Scala, Kyleigh's husband, Penguin. A nickname that didn't seem to bother Bax at all.

He and his brothers had agreed—privately of course—that they approved of the men their sisters had fallen for. Both Reed and Bax could take a joke without getting angry, and even more importantly, they treated their sisters very well. The love they shared was obvious to everyone around them.

The Finnegan brothers couldn't ask for anything better than that.

"Ready to go?" Brady asked, eyeing Shelby and Eva.

"Yes." Shelby looked a little harried after putting Eva's winter coat on. She had the farm animals tucked in her own coat pockets and was carrying Eva's dolly. "We're ready."

"I have to go to the bafroom," Eva announced.

"This way, sweetie." Shelby took her daughter by the hand to lead her outside the conference room to the restrooms. When they returned ten minutes later, Eva appeared ready to go. He hoped that meant swimming was on the back burner for a while.

Aiden knelt beside the little girl. "Can I carry you to the car?"

The little girl shyly nodded. He lifted her into his arms and followed the rest of the family toward the main entrance.

"Wait here," Kyleigh directed. "Brady, you should come out with us and pull the SUV up closer to the door."

"Sure thing." Brady, Kyleigh, and Reed all headed outside, leaving Aiden and Shelby at the doorway.

"I can't believe Oliver Kennedy tried to frame you for Emmitt's death." She looked up at him. "Do you really think Oliver killed him?"

"I do, yes. Using the story to cover up his own crime is the only thing that makes sense. Why else would he sign an affidavit to that effect?"

"Oliver was so nice to me after Emmitt's death," she said quietly. "Brought takeout meals for us on several occasions and offered to babysit Eva." She swallowed hard, then added, "It's difficult to imagine him doing all of that if he was the one to kill Emmitt in the first place."

Sounded to Aiden as if the guy wanted Shelby for himself. Was that it? Was Oliver upset that he was the one who'd taken the role of guarding Shelby? But then why try to kill her?

Maybe the reason the shooter, a.k.a. Kennedy, kept missing was he wanted Shelby to come to him, seeking comfort. The way Parsons had wanted to arrest him would have given Kennedy the chance to step in to be near Shelby.

An intriguing theory, but one they were far from proving.

Brady drove his SUV up to the front door. Both Reed and Kyleigh jogged over to help offer protection as he escorted Shelby outside.

It didn't take long to get situated in the SUV. Brady backed away from the building, then turned to head toward the road. Kyleigh and Reed jumped into their vehicle and quickly pulled out behind them.

As he buckled his seat belt, Aiden silently prayed the trip back to the safe house would be uneventful. Thankfully, Bill Parsons didn't know anything about the place. Which meant the location was a secret from Kennedy too.

When Brady headed due west, he shot his brother a questioning look. "I know you mentioned an alternate route, but we need to go north at some point."

"We will." Brady shrugged. "Sit back and enjoy the scenery."

Easier said than done. Eva was growing cranky, and glancing over his shoulder, he noticed Shelby was looking more and more frazzled too.

Brady broke into song, and thankfully that helped distract the little girl. They all sang along, even though Aiden had to fudge the words. He didn't have a son like Brady and hadn't been exposed to kid's songs.

After thirty minutes of singing, Eva's eyelids began to droop. The adults fell silent, hoping the little girl would take another nap.

Aiden wondered if Rhy was ready for this, considering Devon had just delivered their newborn daughter, Colleen. Which reminded him that they hadn't heard from him in a while.

"I'd like to call Rhy, let him know our progress," he said to Brady.

"Good idea, but don't use the speaker." Brady grinned. "Eva finally fell asleep."

"No problem." He quickly called his oldest brother. "How are Devon and the new baby doing?"

"They're great." Rhy sounded like a tired but proud father. "Colleen is the most beautiful baby in the world. I can't wait for the rest of the family to meet her."

"We want that too," he agreed. Oddly, spending so much time with Shelby and Eva had made him acutely aware of how much Rhy and Tarin had given up to raise the youngest of the siblings. Including him. "I want to give you a brief update."

"I've been thinking about you, Aiden," Rhy said, a hint of regret in his tone. "I feel bad that I haven't been able to help."

"Brady, Reed, Kyleigh, Tarin, and Marc Callahan have us covered. Devon and Colleen need you more than we do."

"Thanks. So what's going on?"

Aiden gave his brother the latest news, including the bit about how Oliver Kennedy was trying to frame him for Emmitt Copeland's murder. And how close he'd come to being arrested by Bill Parsons.

"I'm glad you have truth on your side," Rhy said. "But I'd feel better knowing Kennedy is in custody."

"We don't have any evidence against him, at least not yet." He hoped Strauss would find what they needed and soon. "The biggest issue is that we haven't nailed down his motive for coming after Shelby. The only thing I can come up with is that these attacks were set up to force Shelby into being with Kenney. Especially if I'm out of the way."

"That makes sense, sort of." Rhy sighed. "You may need Tarin's detective brain. I haven't gotten much sleep, so mine is useless."

He laughed. "Never useless, Rhy. Give your wife and daughter a kiss for us. We'll be in touch once we get this wrapped up."

"I like the way you're thinking positive," Rhy said. "Later, Aiden. Stay safe."

"We will." He lowered the phone, glancing at Brady. "What do you think? Should we call Tarin? He stayed to smooth things over with the Timberland Falls PD, and I assume from there he headed home. I'm sure he wouldn't mind coming back."

"I'm not opposed to more brain cells working on this, but Heath is the one with access to the army database. We know for sure this is related to Emmitt Copeland's death." Brady shrugged. "The perp has to be someone within the army or with army connections. I guess it's possible Kennedy or the other guy, was it Morrison?"

"Yeah, Kennedy and Morrison. They were both at the funeral for Shelby's father."

"It could be that Kennedy wants Shelby for himself, but that doesn't seem to be enough." Brady shook his head. "Either one of them is directly involved, or they tipped off the real perp. Strauss should be able to dig further to find out what is motivating this guy to lash out at Shelby now."

"Yeah, okay." The motive was really bugging him. Aiden felt as if there was a giant hole in the puzzle, and the pieces that were left did not fit in any way shape or form.

What were they missing?

After driving for what seemed like an hour, Brady finally turned to head north. They were making a giant circle around the city to get back to the safe house, coming in from a completely opposite direction. He appreciated the extra precautions, but he was also anxious to talk to Heath.

They had to find something more to go on. They just had to!

Shelby and Eva deserved to be safe from harm.

THE LONG CAR ride was making Shelby sleepy. She hadn't gotten that much sleep last night, and the events of the day were wearing her down. Her stomach rumbled with hunger, so she leaned forward to get Aiden's attention. "We might want to bring dinner with us," she suggested. "I'm sure the guys didn't bother to make anything."

"Good point." He glanced at her over his shoulder. "Anything in particular Eva would like?"

"We already had spaghetti, but she wouldn't mind macaroni and cheese, or maybe hot dogs and burgers." She shrugged. "Whatever is easier for the rest of you."

"I'll call in an order from our favorite Italian restaurant," he offered. "They have great lasagna, mac and cheese, garlic bread, and salads."

"That sounds wonderful." She didn't mind burgers, but hot dogs made her want to gag. Unfortunately, Eva loved them.

Most kids did for reasons unknown.

"Make sure you let Reed and Kyleigh know we're making a detour," Brady said.

"Will do." She listened as Aiden placed the order, then called his sister. She was surprised he put it on speaker for her sake. "Kyleigh? We're picking up dinner along the way."

"That's fine. There's no sign of anyone following us," she said. "Looks like smooth sailing now that Parsons is out of the picture."

"Great. See you soon." Aiden lowered his phone when it rang again. He once again put the call on speaker. "Heath, please tell me you have good news."

"I wish I could, but honestly, I have not found anything to link Kennedy to these attacks on Shelby." Heath sounded tired and frustrated. Shelby imagined the investigator had spent the last few hours glued to his computer screen.

She could tell Aiden wasn't happy with that news. "What are we missing?" he asked. "Why would Oliver Kennedy try to frame me for Emmitt's death? Especially if it was ruled an accident?"

"I don't know. He has that one reprimand for sexual harassment. I was able to get the details on that, sounds relatively mild in the big scheme of things. Not that I'm taking it lightly," Heath hastened to add. "Rude comments about how great Justine would look in a bikini aren't appropriate. But he didn't put hands on, which is probably why it was only a minor blip on his record."

Shelby felt a twinge of sympathy for the pretty woman. Men could be so insensitive.

"Okay, thanks." Aiden sighed. "Maybe it's time to switch gears and go back to Bill Parsons. Or even Victor Morrison."

"It could be someone within Parsons's office too," Heath said. "I mean, I know he has an administrative assistant, a woman by the name of Lorna Kline. She's the one who contacted me when Parsons asked to meet with me about taking on the investigation into Mitchell's death."

Aiden abruptly straightened in his seat, glancing back at her for a quick second. "Lorna may have told someone else about the meeting at the FBI offices. Or maybe she's even involved herself."

"It seems odd that she'd want to kill Shelby, but it's very possible she's talking to someone she shouldn't be." The hint of exhaustion in Heath's tone vanished. "I'll dig into her a bit."

"Great. By the way, we're picking up lasagna for dinner."

"I'm glad. Marc was just saying something about ordering out."

"Tell him not to bother. We'll be there soon." Aiden disconnected from the call.

Shelby reached over to touch his shoulder. "There's no way Lorna Kline is involved in this."

He twisted in his seat to face her. "Do you know her?"

"She used to work for my dad but then was moved over to support Bill Parsons." She frowned, thinking back to the offhand comment her father had made about the move. "I remember because there was someone new who answered my dad's phone, and I asked him about it. There didn't seem to be any animosity between them. So why would she have anything to do with this?"

"I'm not saying she does, but she could have said something without realizing the implication of letting that information out," he said mildly.

"Most assistants know how to keep a secret," she protested. "It's part of being vetted to have access to classified information.

"Maybe." He didn't sound convinced.

Brady pulled into the parking lot of what appeared to be several large stores. The Italian restaurant was sandwiched between two big ones.

"Hold on," Brady said as Aiden reached for the door. "Wait for Reed and Kyleigh."

When Reed pulled up next to them, he signaled for Aiden to stay put.

"I'm not helpless," Aiden muttered.

Brady ignored him.

Reed slid out and ran inside the restaurant. He emerged a few minutes later carrying a large white bag and grinning widely. Shelby could almost smell the tangy lasagna and garlic bread from here. Reed took a moment to store the food in the back seat before jumping back behind the wheel. Seconds later, they were back on the road.

"There's no way Lorna is involved," Shelby repeated. She didn't want Aiden to waste time going down that road. "I keep thinking of how Oliver tried to befriend me after Emmitt's death. Maybe there was something more driving him to be there for us. Like guilt."

"That could be." He glanced back at her. "But it can't hurt to rule Lorna out anyway."

"Mommy?" Eva woke up, rubbing her eyes with her fists. "I'm hungry."

"We're having macaroni and cheese for dinner." Shelby injected enthusiasm into her tone. "Doesn't that sound good?"

The little girl nodded and went back to playing with her farm animals. Shelby was anxious to get back to the safe house. The trip to the FBI office had been more than any of them had bargained for.

Fifteen minutes later, Brady turned onto the street where the place was located. Shelby noticed they were coming in from the opposite direction from before. Brady had taken so many turns that she'd been completely lost. Especially since she wasn't familiar with this area.

It looked as if the sidewalk leading to the front door had been shoveled recently. Brady pulled into the driveway and killed the engine.

Shelby unlatched her seatbelt, then went to work on Eva's car seat straps.

"We should wait for Reed and Kyleigh," Brady said as Aiden pushed his door open. "They ended up a few car lengths back as rush-hour traffic picked up."

"We're fine," Aiden said. "Marc is only a few feet away."

He opened the back passenger door to pick up Eva. But now her daughter wasn't having it. She twisted away, holding her arms out to Shelby. "Mommy."

"Sorry. She gets clingy sometimes after her nap." Shelby took the little girl in her arms and slid out the other door. A woman carrying a baby came rushing over from the driveway directly across the street. There was a blue SUV parked near the end of the driveway.

"Can you help me? I'm locked out of the house." The dark-haired woman seemed frazzled, and Shelby could relate. Kids could be trying even when there wasn't a crisis, like being locked out.

"Of course." Shelby hurried toward the woman. "Oh, your little boy is so cute. How old is he?"

"He's eighteen months old." The dark-haired woman's smile faded as she slipped her hand from her pocket revealing a small gun. Shelby sucked in a harsh breath when the woman aimed it at her chest. Aiden must have moved closer because the stranger said, "Stay back, Finnegan, or I'll shoot!"

Shoot? Who was this woman? Shelby stared at her in horror, wondering what on earth was going on. They were both holding small, innocent children. What was she thinking? Especially pulling a gun on her?

But then the woman's features clicked in her memory. She remembered seeing this woman's face on the computer screen. It took a moment to place the name.

Jane Fordham. The woman who had gone dark eighteen months ago after going out on medical leave to have her baby.

"What do you want, Jane?" She pushed the question

through her tight throat. "There's no sense in shooting me here. Not with so many witnesses."

"Stay back!" Jane's eyes were wild, her entire demeanor seemed to be on the edge. "You deserve to die. I'm not giving up, not now. My son, Emmitt, should have the army benefits you and your brat are getting."

The words sank deep. Her earlier suspicions were confirmed. The little boy in this woman's arms was her husband's son.

# CHAPTER FIFTEEN

Aiden couldn't believe Jane Fordham had found the safe house. And that she was holding a gun on Shelby and Eva while carrying her own son. Who did that? The woman was mentally unbalanced.

And that made her extremely dangerous.

"You don't want to shoot me," Shelby said in a calm voice. "I understand why you're upset. Emmitt shouldn't have left you high and dry with a son to raise."

"Our son!" Jane screeched. Her face twisted with hate. "Emmitt didn't love you, he loved me!"

"I know he did." He admired Shelby's ability to speak calmly while staring down the barrel of a gun. "I'm sure we can work something out. I agree your son deserves financial support. I'll do whatever I can to help you, but you need to put the gun down first."

"Work something out?" Jane let out a harsh laugh. "It's too late for that."

Aiden didn't like the sound of that. He worried she would pull a murder suicide if they didn't intervene. He didn't dare take his gaze off Jane Fordham, while praying

Kyleigh and Reed would get there and find a way to help him disarm the woman. It wouldn't be easy, not with her gun so close to Shelby and Eva. If they startled her, Jane could fire off two rounds before they could stop her.

She was, after all, a trained soldier. Maybe slightly rusty, having been out of action since giving birth, but still competent in using a weapon.

He estimated the distance between him and Jane to be roughly six feet. It felt more like six miles. Especially considering how Shelby and Eva were much closer to her. Impossible for him to cover the distance in time.

But that wouldn't stop him if this situation deteriorated any further. He had to pray that Shelby would find cover.

"Please, Jane. Put the gun away. You don't want to risk harming Emmitt, do you? We're both mothers, right? We would do anything to protect our children."

"Emmitt didn't protect us," Jane said in a low, agonizing tone. Aiden felt a flicker of compassion for what she must be going through. Not that it gave her an excuse to kill. The barrel of the gun in her hand dipped for a second, then steadied. "And that means I have to take what's rightfully mine."

"You can't collect money if you're in jail," Shelby said, a hint of desperation in her tone, as if the tense situation was getting to her. "Don't you see? I have an FBI agent standing behind me. If you kill me, they'll kill you, and Emmitt will end up in foster care, growing up without either of his parents. Is that what you want for him?"

A flicker of movement from behind Jane caught Aiden's eye. He tried not to shift his gaze to the point he drew Jane's attention. But he felt certain Kyleigh and Reed were behind her.

Yet even though he was thrilled to have additional

backup, Shelby and Eva were still too close to Jane and the barrel of her gun.

"I told you it's too late!" Jane's voice rose in agitation. "Things have gone too far."

"It's never too late," Shelby said. "I promise we'll find a way out of this. But you really need to put the gun down."

"Jane, don't!" Jane startled when a male voice shouted from somewhere off to the right. Jane turned that way. Aiden rushed forward, practically leaping in front of Shelby and Eva. As if they'd choreographed it, Shelby threw herself into a snowbank, clutching Eva to her chest and using her own body to shield the little girl.

The gun fired just as Aiden slammed his arm against Jane's, the bullet going harmlessly up into the sky. The eighteen-month-old baby cried out as he slipped from her arms. Aiden tackled Jane, wincing as the young boy came down with them. He hoped the snow-covered ground prevented him from being hurt.

"No, Jane!" A man Aiden belatedly recognized as Victor Morrison ran toward them. His gaze was etched in horror as if he hadn't anticipated this turn of events.

"Stay back!" Brady barked. "FBI, stay back and keep your hands where I can see them!"

Victor stopped, his expression resigned as Kyleigh and Reed approached from either side with their weapons drawn.

Aiden rolled off Jane, searching for the gun. When he found it, he put his foot on top, shoving it deeper into the snow, then reached for the young boy. "Hey there, it's okay. Your mommy is fine."

She wasn't fine, but he needed to calm the toddler down. Emmitt junior reared away from Aiden, reaching his arms toward Victor.

"May I take him?" Victor asked. "Please? I'm the only father figure he's ever known."

"Don't move," Reed said. "You don't get the kid until I pat you down."

Victor lifted his arms out from his sides, allowing Reed to search him for a weapon. Of course, the guy had a gun and a knife, as most soldiers did. Reed made a point of checking for an ankle weapon, but there wasn't one. Then he stepped back. "Okay, he can take the kid."

Since Emmitt was crying loud enough to break eardrums, Aiden gratefully handed the boy to Victor. Then he turned his attention to Jane, who was curled in a ball on the ground, sobbing uncontrollably.

"Get up." He reached down to grasp her arm. "You're under arrest for attempted murder." He didn't mention the murder of Tom Mitchell because he wasn't sure which of these two had pulled the trigger.

"This is my fault," Victor said in a low voice. "I tried to protect Jane, but she was fixated on Shelby and her daughter."

"Are you and Jane married?" Aiden hauled Jane to her feet. Despite her earlier bravado, the woman continued sobbing into her hands, going along without a fight now that it was finally over.

"No!" Victor looked appalled. "I could never—Jane is my *stepsister*."

Aiden didn't remember anything about a stepsister, but he'd been more focused on Oliver Kennedy. And blood relatives to their key suspects. Which just showed how far off track they'd gone.

"Did you kill Tom Mitchell?" Aiden asked, shooting Victor a narrow look.

The soldier glanced away, swallowing hard. "It wasn't me."

"Jane, then?" he pressed.

"I honestly don't know. This is more complicated than you realize," Victor said in a low voice. "I've been trying to support Jane through this, but she hasn't been listening. She had a promising career working in army communications until she got pregnant."

"Who then?" he demanded, filing away the information on Jane's having a communications background. "I need to know who killed Tom Mitchell?"

"I did." Another voice had Aiden spinning around. He shouldn't have been surprised to see Bill Parsons standing there. The sergeant major held up his hands as if in surrender. "I knew what Emmitt Copeland had done, how he'd had an affair and gotten Jane Fordham pregnant. I tried to cover it up, but then Greg Savage started digging into things, and well . . ." His voice trailed off.

"Stay right there," Brady said. "Reed, hold him at gunpoint until I frisk him."

"Go ahead," Parsons said in a resigned tone. "The FBI took my weapon and refused to give it back until their investigation was complete."

Aiden remembered Donovan saying that but waited until Brady did the search, then stepped back. "He's not armed."

"You killed your own investigator?" Aiden could hardly believe what he was hearing. "Why would you cover up for Emmitt?"

There was a long pause. Then Parsons said, "I am—was Emmitt's father. His mother and I never married, so Emmitt didn't know it. I—we kept it a secret from him."

A hushed silence fell over the group. Again, Aiden had

to admit he had not seen that one coming. Bill Parsons was baby Emmitt's grandfather. What a tangled web of secrets. All leading to violence. "So why are you here now?"

The old man grimaced. "I heard from my boss that the FBI had gotten a subpoena for my personnel and financial records." He darted a glance at Brady and shrugged. "Donovan and your brother are smart. I knew it wouldn't take long for them to put the pieces together. I made child support payments to Emmitt's mother until he was eighteen." Parsons's gaze shifted to the baby in Victor's arms. "When I discovered what had happened, and how Jane had fallen into the same situation, I wanted to protect her. But then I discovered how fixated she was on Ms. Copeland and her daughter." He paused, then added, "I came forward now because Jane isn't a bad person. She needs help. And if I take responsibility for my actions, she and Emmitt stand a better chance of getting the help they need."

Aiden blew out a breath as he digested this. It seemed Bill Parsons was going out on a limb to protect his grandson. Maybe because he hadn't been there for his own son, other than providing financial support. "What about Tim Tobin's attack on us?"

"I ordered him to do it." Parsons dropped his gaze. "I kept thinking if you were all out of the way, I could cover this all up and move forward with Jane and Emmitt."

"You killed your own investigator and set up another former soldier to kill us." Aiden struggled to find any sympathy for the guy. "You don't deserve those stripes on your sleeve."

Parsons didn't respond.

"Did you ask Kevin Carter to call me about my dad's files?" Shelby asked.

"Yes." Parsons shrugged. "I suspected he was digging

into Emmitt's past too. I didn't want your father to know about Jane and Emmitt."

"Did you kill my father?" Shelby demanded.

"What? No." Parsons looks shocked by that. "He died of a heart attack."

Aiden wasn't sure he believed the guy, but there would be time to dig into that further later. For now, they had Parsons on murder.

"Okay, then." Brady stepped forward with handcuffs. "Bill Parsons, you are under arrest for the murder of Tom Mitchell." His brother went on to recite the entire Miranda warning, even though Parsons had already confessed, and in front of several cop witnesses.

"I can take him in," Marc offered. He must have come out of the safe house at some point, but Aiden hadn't noticed him until now.

"We can take Jane into custody too," Reed offered. "I think a good lawyer will argue extreme emotional disturbance, but she still threatened Shelby and Eva with a gun, as well as taking several other shots at them, so we can't let her walk." Reed glanced at Victor Morrison. "You'll need to take care of Emmitt while we get her processed through the system."

"I understand." Victor turned to Jane, his expression earnest. "I'll hire you the best lawyer money can buy, okay? Don't say anything more, Jane. Not a single word."

Jane nodded listlessly as if she no longer cared what happened to her. Aiden couldn't help wondering if she was battling depression or some other mental illness.

"Wait, one more thing." Aiden stepped toward Bill Parsons. "Did Oliver Kennedy really sign an affidavit that I killed Copeland?"

Parsons shrugged. "He did, but only on my orders. I had

another female soldier come forward with sexual harassment complaints against Kennedy. I told him to sign the document or get booted out of the army with a dishonorable discharge. He signed them."

"Does that mean Emmitt's death really was an accident?" Shelby asked. When Parsons didn't answer, she took a step toward him. "After everything me and my daughter have been through, I deserve to know the truth."

"Yes, Mitchell deemed it an accident, and I believe he was right." Parsons suddenly looked like an old man. "I was angry and wanted to pin Emmitt's death on someone, anyone. But Mitchell insisted that other than the rumor of an affair, there was nothing to support his death as anything but accidental. Since I knew about the affair, I let it go. But then he started digging into Emmitt's background, and I couldn't allow the truth to come out."

Shelby nodded and moved closer to Aiden. He reached out to put his arm around her shoulders, drawing her close. Marc Callahan asked Brady if he could use the SUV to take Parsons in. Brady nodded in agreement. Kyleigh and Reed were going to use their vehicle to take Jane Fordham away.

"Oh, by the way, you need the food." His sister sighed. "I was so looking forward to that lasagna and garlic bread."

"Me too," Reed said with a frown.

"We'll save some for you." Aiden gestured to the safe house. "Come back here when you're finished. We may as well eat here before heading back."

"Deal," Kyleigh said. "We'll return as soon as we can. Come with us, Ms. Fordham."

Reed picked up Jane's weapon and tucked it into his glove to protect her fingerprints, then followed. Aiden watched as Kyleigh and Reed escorted Jane Fordham to their vehicle, which they'd parked a few blocks down the road from the safe house. Kyleigh returned with the large bag of food, handing it over.

"Thanks, Kyleigh. For everything." He took the bag from her fingers. "Tell Clark thanks too."

She rolled her eyes at the nickname but hurried back to join Reed. "Don't forget to save us some," she called back over her shoulder.

Victor turned away, carrying Emmitt Junior.

"Wait!" Shelby pulled away from him and hurried over to him. "I, uh, this is Eva." She smiled tentatively at Victor. "She's Emmitt's half sister."

"Yes, I know." Victor managed a smile. "Eva is a pretty name."

"Thank you. Eva, this is Emmitt." Shelby introduced her daughter to the little boy. "Can you say Emmitt?"

"Mit," Eva said. "Hi, Mit."

Emmitt hid his face against Victor's neck. "Sorry," Victor said. "Emmitt is feeling shy today."

Watching Shelby interact with her husband's illegitimate son made his heart swell with love. No matter how upset she was about what her husband had done, it was clear Shelby would not hold the father's sins against his son. If he hadn't already loved Shelby and Eva, he would have fallen hard in that sweet moment.

Yet he didn't believe Shelby felt the same way toward him. And really, he couldn't blame her. She and Eva deserved to return to their normal, quiet life in Oshkosh.

A life he would never ask her to leave behind.

---

SHELBY'S HEART ached for what would happen to Emmitt's son now that Jane had been taken into custody. It wasn't easy to think about how her husband had cheated on her, fathering a child with another woman, but that was hardly the little boy's fault. And she wanted Eva to know her half brother and vice versa. She met Victor's gaze. "I hope we can get the two kids together again sometime."

"Ah, maybe." Victor flushed. "I don't know how Jane will feel about that, but we'll see how things go."

"Okay." She took a step backward. "Just know I'd like Eva to know her brother."

"That's nice of you," Victor said. "I'm sorry for all of this. I guess I should have reported Jane's obsession sooner."

"Wait. You knew she was coming after me?" That sparked her anger. "Do you realize how close she came to shooting me and Eva?"

"I didn't know, not right away . . ." He grimaced. "But the way she kept leaving Emmitt with me raised my suspicions. I found the jammer in her car, and she claimed she was just testing it. Then I caught up with her earlier today after she fired at your SUV at the train tracks. She promised me she'd go home after that but didn't."

"How did she know we were there?" Shelby held Victor's gaze as Aiden came up to stand beside her. "From Parsons?"

Victor took a step back, too, as if sensing he was on shaky ground. "Jane spoke to Parsons on a regular basis. He tended to act like a mentor to her. She mentioned to me that Parsons was planning to have Finnegan arrested, but then he told Jane the meeting didn't go as planned." He paused, then added, "I followed her here. You know the rest. I didn't do anything illegal."

"That's not true," Aiden said. "You should have reported Jane to the police for shooting at our SUV. That's reckless endangerment."

"Yeah, well, no one was hurt, so I concentrated on getting Jane out of there." Victor lifted his chin. "You want to arrest me? Go ahead. But Emmitt will end up in foster care."

Shelby couldn't stand the thought. "Let it go for now, Aiden."

"He holds some responsibility for this," he protested.

"I know, but he didn't pull the trigger. Jane did. I'm satisfied in knowing the danger is over." She turned to look up at him. "Please? Just let it go."

She could tell he didn't want to, but he nodded at Victor. "Take the kid home. But know this, your career in the army is over. We won't take legal action as a civilian, but you can be held responsible within the army. You can either resign or I'll make sure you're brought up on charges of dishonorable conduct."

"I was planning to resign anyway to better support Jane and Emmitt." Victor turned and hurried back to the SUV parked at the end of the driveway across the road. It didn't take long for him to drive away.

She let out her breath in a soundless sigh. It was over. For good.

"Are you okay?" Aiden asked, his dark eyes full of concern. "That was a lot to handle."

"We're fine." She bent over to set Eva on the driveway. Her daughter went to the closest snowbank to grab a handful of snow. "I prayed the entire time Jane held that gun on me. I expected her to shoot at any moment. If Victor hadn't shown up to distract her when he had . . ."

"I know. Me too." Aiden pulled her into his arms. She eagerly hugged him back, her eyes brimming with tears. Why now, she had no idea. Maybe they were tears of relief.

Or tears of sadness over the troubled future baby Emmitt faced.

Or maybe they filled her eyes because she didn't want to say goodbye to Aiden.

"Hey, are you crying?" Aiden's voice sounded panicked. "Don't cry. You're safe and so is Eva. Everything is fine. We can head to your home in Oshkosh after we eat dinner. You can even teach on Monday if you're up to it."

She shook her head, trying to pull herself together. "I— it's just everything. So many lies and deceit." Her gaze landed on Eva playing gleefully in the snow. "Lives that will be changed forever." Including hers, she silently added.

"I'm sorry you've had to go through this." Aiden pressed a kiss to her hair. He was the kindest, most honorable man she'd ever known. "I'll support you, Shelby. I can take a leave of absence and help you and Eva work through things."

"You would, wouldn't you?" She couldn't help but smile. "You have your own family to deal with Aiden. We are not your responsibility."

"What if I said I wanted you to be my responsibility?" His gaze searched hers. "I'm going to leave the National Guard, Shelby. I was feeling restless before this happened, and I realize now that I can't go back."

"I hate that you're giving up your career over this." The thought troubled her.

"Like I said, my heart wasn't in it." He tugged her close. "I know this may be too soon for you, and if so, I under- stand, but I love you, Shelby. I would like you to give me a chance to prove how much."

"Love?" She wasn't sure she heard him correctly. "In a few short days? That's impossible."

To her surprise, he chuckled. "Obviously, you haven't

met my family. Or heard how they all found the love of their lives in a short period of time. One thing about the Finnegans, we know what we want." His gaze softened. "I know it's too soon for you. And that's okay. Just give me a chance. Let me move to Oshkosh. When my tour of duty is over, I'll find a job. Maybe as a cop."

She stared at him in awe. "You would move away from your family for me?"

"Yes." There was no hesitation in his tone. "I would do anything for you, Shelby."

She wanted desperately to believe him. To trust his love. But she'd dated Emmitt for nine months before saying the words, "I love you."

"Really?" His brown eyes widened, making her realize she'd said the words out loud.

"Yes, really." She smiled. "But you're right about needing some time, Aiden. I—can't rush into anything. Eva doesn't deserve to have her life turned upside down if things between us don't work out."

"I would never hurt you or Eva. I'm in this for the long haul so take all the time you need, Shelby. I'm not going anywhere. All I ask is that you give me a chance."

Before she could say anything more, he captured her mouth in a deep kiss. One that was even more powerful than before because her love for him washed over her.

She loved him! God had brought Aiden into her life when she'd needed him the most.

Yet she would take the time he'd offered, for her daughter's sake. And because these last few days had been a whirlwind of danger.

But deep down she knew Aiden Finnegan was the man for her.

A snowball lightly smacked her in the back. Aiden

broke off the kiss and laughed as Eva threw another snow-ball at them. She turned to scold the little girl, but her daughter giggled so hard she couldn't do it.

"I got you, Mommy! I got you!"

"You sure did." She was glad Eva was too small to make a real snowball. She bent and made her own, lobbing it toward Eva who screamed in delight and ran away.

Aiden joined the fun, making a much bigger and harder snowball. She narrowed her gaze in warning. He simply grinned and hit her in the chest with the snowball.

"That's it, you're getting one too." She quickly scooped up another handful of snow. She hit him on the back of his head. She'd been aiming for his back and braced herself for his anger.

He turned to grin at her. "Good one."

"Hey, break it up out there," Brady called from the front door. "This isn't playtime. Your lasagna and macaroni and cheese is getting cold!"

"Macaroni and cheese?" Eva perked up. "I'm hungry, Mommy!"

"Me too." Shelby took her daughter's hand. Aiden stepped over to take the other one. The three of them walked inside the safe house.

Together.

# EPILOGUE

*Thanksgiving Day...*

Aiden glanced at Shelby as he pulled into the driveway of the homestead. She'd met most of his siblings before, but this would be her first time meeting the entire crew. Well, most of them anyway. Reed was working today and so was Tarin. But Tarin's wife, Joy, would be there and so would the newest member of the Finnegan family, Colleen Finnegan, Rhy and Devon's daughter.

"Ready?"

She slanted him a look. "Should I be worried?"

"Not at all. They're going to love you and Eva." He glanced back at the little girl who was playing with a new doll, one that cried when tilted a certain way. Eva loved making the dolly cry, which made for a long ride.

Not that he was complaining. He hoped one day to adopt Eva as his own. Well, once he convinced Shelby to marry him.

It had only been two and a half weeks since their lives had returned to normal. Or their new normal. Jane

Fordham was being held in a psychiatric facility after the jammer was found in her car, linking her to the attack outside the homestead. She was getting the care she needed and was still facing charges for reckless endangerment. He and Shelby prayed for her often, for baby Emmitt's sake.

Parsons was being held in Leavenworth without bail.

Aiden had found an apartment in Oshkosh, sold his cherry red truck for a family friendly SUV and spent every minute he wasn't working for the National Guard with Shelby and Eva. They had become incredibly important to him in a very short amount of time. Similar to the way his siblings had fallen in love, he'd thought with a wry smile.

"Let's do it." Shelby pushed her door open.

He opened the back passenger door to unbuckle Eva. The little girl lifted her arms so he could carry her. Every time she did that, his heart somersaulted in his chest.

As they headed up the walkway to the front door, it opened revealing Elly. "Aiden! Shelby! Eva! We're so happy you're here!"

"Give them some room, El," Alanna said. Because of their different schedules and the hour-long drive, his twin hadn't met Shelby yet. "Hi, Shelby and Eva. Welcome to the Finnegan homestead."

"Thank you for inviting us to spend the holiday with you." Shelby held out her hand to Alanna. "I recognize you from Aiden's description. You're just as beautiful as he said you were."

"He said that?" Alanna cocked a brow. "Usually he's not that nice."

"Hey, what do you mean?" He protested as he set Eva on the floor. She clung to his leg in a moment of shyness. "I'm always nice."

"You gave Reed the nickname Clark," Alanna retorted. "That wasn't nice."

"Better than Penguin," Kyleigh said, joining them. "Although Bax loves penguins now, go figure."

Shelby waded farther into the room, where even more Finnegans waited. Once they'd taken off their winter coats, he brought Shelby close to his side. "I'll introduce you but don't feel obligated to remember everyone's names. It's a lot."

"Oh, I think I can handle it." She surprised him by pointing them out, going through the group that had gathered together. "Rhy, Devon, and their new daughter, Colleen. Joy who is pregnant and married to Tarin, Bax and Kyleigh, Brady, Grace, and their son, Caleb." She paused, then continued. "Sami and Quinn, Colin and Faye, Alanna who is engaged to Reed who is also not here, and Elly."

There was a long moment of silence before his siblings broke into wild applause. "Wow, Aiden, she rocked it!" Quinn said in awe.

"Did you quiz her the entire ride down from Oshkosh?" Colin demanded. "I think you must have."

"I didn't!" Although he was impressed Shelby had thought to memorize everyone as he'd described them. Having met many of them also helped.

"I think it's sweet how Shelby took the time to get to know us," Elly said. "She's a keeper, Aiden."

He'd asked Rhy not to put too much pressure on his showing up with Shelby and Eva, explaining briefly how she needed time before committing to anything. Apparently, Elly didn't get the memo.

Or more likely, she ignored it. Elly had a sweet, kind heart, and he knew she hoped he and Shelby would get engaged.

At this point, he was just grateful to be seeing Shelby and Eva on a regular basis. No matter how much he loved her, he wasn't going to push for anything more. Not until she was ready.

Maybe by this time next year they'd be able to announce their engagement.

"Welcome to the craziness, Shelby," Alanna said with a smile. "It's nice to know how well you fit in with the Finnegans."

He shot Rhy a helpless glance, silently asking him to tell the sibs to back off.

"Thank you, Alanna." Shelby gazed around the room. "I want each of you to know how much I love Aiden. And that I hope someday we can eventually move back to the area so that he isn't separated from all of you."

*Wait, what?* Aiden gaped. "Whoa, when did you decide this?"

"Which? That I love you or that we should eventually move back here?" Shelby's eyes twinkled. "After meeting just a few of your family members, I knew it wouldn't be right to keep you so far from them. But I need to finish off the school semester in Oshkosh."

"Hey, there's no rush, remember?" A weird wave of panic hit hard. Had Elly reached out to Shelby without his knowing about it? Or maybe Alanna? "I promised to give you time."

"And you did." Shelby stepped closer and slipped her arm around his waist. "My feelings for you aren't going to change, Aiden. I love you."

"I love you too." He lowered his mouth to kiss her.

"I knew it!" Elly exclaimed. "I knew they were perfect for each other."

He reluctantly lifted his head to find everyone's eyes on them. Colleen started to cry, which broke up the poignant moment.

"Excuse me," Devon murmured. "I think she's hungry."

"So am I," Colin complained. "Isn't it time for turkey soon?"

"Watch out, or I'll stab your hand with a fork again," Aiden warned. That made everyone laugh.

Grace introduced Caleb to Eva, and they were soon playing together with several toys Grace and Brady had brought along.

"You chose well, Aiden," Rhy said in a low voice.

"I'm very blessed," he agreed. Then he glanced at Elly. "Eight down and one to go. What do you think, Rhy?"

His eldest sibling scowled. "Elly's too young to be thinking about settling down. I'm not even convinced she likes her job as an EMT. I'm glad you've found Shelby and Eva and that you have a new career path in mind. But I'm still worried about Elly. We need to convince her to do something else with her life. If that's what she wants."

Aiden nodded. "I agree, Elly deserves to be happy too." And as he watched the youngest Finnegan, he caught a glimpse of happiness intermixed with longing in her eyes. But then it was gone as Elly laughed at something the kids were saying. She plopped down beside them, picking up an action figure and joining in.

Shelby came back to stand beside him. She stood on her tiptoes to give him a quick kiss. "I love your family," she whispered.

"And I love you." He pulled her close and silently thanked God for bringing Shelby and Eva into his life.

The family he hadn't even known he'd wanted.

.   .   .

I HOPE you enjoyed Aiden and Shelby's story in *Strategic Threat*. Are you ready for Elly and Joe's story in *Christmas Crisis*? Click here!

# DEAR READER

Thanks so much for reading my Finnegan First Responder series. I'm truly blessed to have wonderful readers like you. And I've had so much fun bringing the Callahans back to help their Finnegan cousins!

I hope you stick with me for Elly and Joe's story in *Christmas Crisis*. I have been plotting this book in my mind since I started the series, and of course, there will be a family reunion with the Callahans at the end. Just in time for Christmas! Don't forget, you can purchase eBooks or audiobooks directly from my website will receive a 15% discount by using the code **LauraScott15**.

I adore hearing from my readers! I can be found through my website at https://www.laurascottbooks.com, via Facebook at https://www.facebook.com/LauraScott Books, Instagram at https://www.instagram.com/laurascott books/, and Twitter https://twitter.com/laurascottbooks. Also, take a moment to sign up for my monthly newsletter to learn about my new book releases! All subscribers receive a free novella not available for purchase on any platform.

Until next time,
Laura Scott
PS Read on for a sneak peek of *Christmas Crisis*.

# CHRISTMAS CRISIS

## Chapter One

Elly Finnegan looked up in awe at the twinkling blue Christmas lights lining the parade route through downtown Milwaukee. This was her favorite time of year, and more so since she had planned a family reunion between her siblings and their Callahan cousins on Christmas Day. She'd found her grandmother's diary in the attic and couldn't wait to share what she'd learned with the rest of the family. The Callahans and Finnegans shared the same set of great-grandparents, but their respective grandmother siblings had lost touch with each other.

And now she knew why.

Since she was looking upward, she didn't notice the guy coming toward her until she'd bumped into him. Flustered, she smiled and said, "Oh, excuse me."

His gaze sliced toward her. Her smile faded at the hard coldness reflected in his eyes. Elly genuinely loved people, and animals too, having made a habit of bring strays home when she was younger, but there was something about this man that made the hairs on the back of her neck stand up in alarm. He wore a long dark coat that went to his knees, his hands tucked out of sight. Their gazes locked for a long uncomfortable moment before he turned away and merged into the crowd without saying a word.

*Evil.* The word flashed in her mind, a weird sense of impending doom washing over her. But then she told herself not to be ridiculous. Tugging on her boxy navy-blue EMT uniform, she quickly made her way toward the ambulance. She and her EMT partner, Derek, were on duty for the Christmas parade. It was a bit of a relief to Elly as the parade usually went off every year without a hitch. It wasn't likely she and Derek would have to deal with any actual injuries.

Okay, maybe she was getting better at dealing with her irrational aversion to blood, but there was still that moment of lightheadedness that she couldn't quite shake. Between that and the nausea that rolled through her abdomen, she'd barely managed to hold herself together the handful of times she'd been forced to deal with a bleeding injury.

Normally, she spent her days transferring patients from one location to the next. The ambulance company she worked for had contracts with most of the hospitals and nursing homes in the area. It wasn't exciting work by any stretch of the imagination, but she'd been deeply grateful for the uneventful transfers.

She really, really needed to find a way to push through this. The Finnegan family was all about being first responders, and she was bound and determined to do her part. She'd already disappointed her oldest brother, Rhy, after failing first to become a cop, then again when she'd dropped out of the nursing program.

This career she'd chosen would work. It had to. There wasn't another option.

Crowds of people packed both sides of the street along the parade route. She pushed through the throng, smiling at the memory of how her parents had taken her to the Christmas parade when she was young. Her parents had passed away eleven years ago now, and she still missed them. Although she was also grateful for her two oldest brothers, Rhy and Tarin, who'd stepped in to raise her after their tragic loss. As the youngest of nine siblings, she knew she was the main reason Rhy and Tarin had given up having a personal life to move back to the Finnegan homestead. Granted, the twins, Aiden and Alanna, had only been seventeen to her fourteen, but still. She knew full well she had been the driving force behind their decision.

Thankfully, all her older siblings had found love in the past year. She was thrilled with the expansion of the Finnegan clan, including baby Colleen, the newest member of the family, born a few weeks ago to Rhy and Devon. Joy's baby was due next April, and she had a feeling it wouldn't take long for the rest of the family to add to the Finnegan clan. Aiden and Shelby were getting married mid-January, so they had that momentous occasion to look forward to as well.

Glancing at her watch, she realized the parade was about to start. It would take about fifteen minutes or so for the parade to pass by her current location.

"There you are," Derek said. He was three years younger than her twenty-four, although her birthday was only a few weeks away. He'd asked her out, but she'd declined, not having any interest in him. Nice enough guy, but she'd been fighting a crush on Joe Kingsley—a cop who worked for her brother Rhy on the tactical team for months now.

Not that Joe knew she existed. Well, other than being Rhy's youngest sister. He all but patted her head like she was ten every time they met. She shook off the depressing thought.

"This is going to be awesome." Their position near the intersection was such that she'd have a great view of the parade.

"If we don't freeze to death," Derek muttered, stamping his feet and tucking his hands under his armpits. While she had to fight her aversion to blood while working, Derek had grown up in Arizona and hated, absolutely hated the cold weather.

Why he didn't just go back to Arizona was a mystery.

She caught a glimpse of a tall cop, and her heart gave a silly thump when she realized Joe was here too. Obviously working, the way she was. She stepped forward, but then forced herself to stop. She couldn't just rush over to say hi. Not while they were both on duty.

Especially since Joe had never hinted at having any sort of feelings toward her. She was nothing more than a pesky younger sister to him. Tolerated only because Rhy often put Joe in charge of the tactical unit. The sooner she accepted that fact, the better.

Christmas music rang out, indicating the parade had begun. She couldn't help grinning like a little kid as the marching band gave a rousing rendition of Frosty the Snow-man. She sang along, letting out a quick laugh.

The music grew louder as the marching band and the rest of the parade made their way down the street toward them. Elves tossed Christmas candy into the crowd, and a large float on a flatbed trailer had a pair of ice skaters dressed in cheerful red costumes doing twirls on the small patch of ice.

"Oh, that's so cool!" She was impressed the couple was able to spin and skate on a very small ice pond. When the male skater lifted the female over his head, she gasped and applauded along with the rest of the spectators.

*Crack! Crack!* It took a moment for her to realize the skaters were lying on the ice, bleeding.

Gunfire? Had that really been gunfire?

Screams reverberated around her. The marching band scattered. More bullets were fired, and people around her fell to the ground, not moving. *Dear Lord Jesus, no!*

*There was an active shooter at the parade!*

"Get down!" Derek tugged on her arm, trying to get her closer to the shelter of the ambulance. But when she saw Joe and several other cops rushing into danger, she surprised herself by breaking free of Derek's grip.

She grabbed the first aid kit and ran out to where she saw a young kid, barely eight years old, lying on the ground. Bile rushed into her throat, and her head spun as she saw he'd been shot in the leg.

*Don't faint! Don't faint!* She knelt beside the child, but then as more gunfire rang out, she realized she couldn't stay there with him. Instead, she scooped him into her arms and ran stumbling back to the ambulance.

"Here, take care of him!" She thrust the crying boy into Derek's arms. "Go inside the rig!"

Derek nodded and opened the back doors to carry the boy inside. She spun and ran back out into the street where the parade had abruptly stopped.

Her gaze landed on a cop sprawled on the ground on the other side of the street. Joe? *No, please, Lord, no!* Elly scooped up her abandoned first aid kit and darted through the screaming mass of people, nearly tripping over a tuba lying in the street in her haste to reach the fallen officer.

Not Joe, but a familiar face. She searched her memory for his name as she avoided looking down at the massive pool of blood forming beneath him. Kyle. That's right, his name was Kyle.

"Elly?" He stared up at her, confusion in his eyes. As if he didn't understand what was going on. Frankly, she didn't either.

"I'm here. You're going to be okay." The edges of her vision blurred, and she had to tell herself again not to faint. *Not now! Please, Lord, not now!*

"El . . ." He tried to say something more, but then his eyes closed, and his body went limp.

Why was this happening? Her fingers fumbled on the first aid kit as she searched for gauze. As if the small amount she carried could stem the flow of blood running like a river across the frozen street. She swallowed hard, praying she wouldn't be sick. She pressed gauze to his groin wound, but instantly, it was soaked in blood. No use. It was no use!

"Elly!" It took a moment for her name to register. Dazed, she glanced up to see Joe making a beeline toward her, a look of panic etched on his features. Over his shoulder, she saw a man wearing a long dark coat standing above the others. He lifted a long automatic rifle.

"Down!" She screamed the word as loud as she could. Joe reacted instantly, as if she were Rhy shouting an order, and hit the ground as another crack of gunfire rang out. She watched in horror as Joe rolled over, lifted his own weapon, and returned fire.

The guy in the long coat ducked, then took off. She rose to her feet, stumbling toward Joe. "He's getting away!"

"Go back to the ambulance." Joe looked as if he wanted

to stay with her but turned and ran toward the location the shooter had last been, talking into his radio as he went, no doubt putting the other officers in the area on alert to help him search. People were still screaming, some running away, others cradling injured loved ones close.

The entire scene was surreal and straight out of a horror flick. The amount of blood was paralyzing, but Elly forced herself to do her job.

The way Joe was.

Slightly calmer now that she knew the gunman had left the scene, she turned back to Kyle. When she couldn't feel a pulse, she forced herself to move on to the next victim. In times of a crisis, there was no time to waste on those who had no chance of survival. Not when there were so many other victims to assess and treat.

The next closest victim was a young woman being held by a man who was likely her husband. The woman was bleeding from an upper chest wound, but she still had a pulse. Despite being pale and in shock, the woman glanced at her. "Hurts."

"I know." Elly crouched beside them, using more gauze and pressing it against the exit wound. "Hold this," she instructed. The dazed man did as she instructed. "You're going to be okay. Let's get you up and over to the ambulance."

The man looked grateful for something constructive to do. She stood and helped him lift the injured woman. "Hang on to me, Lisa," he instructed.

"I don't understand," Lisa murmured, as if there was a way to make sense out of this horrible act of violence. "Why, Dan? Why?"

"I don't know." He pressed a kiss to her temple and half carried her across the street to the ambulance. There were other victims there now, too, having instinctively gone to the closest source of aid. Derek had the young boy inside but was now kneeling beside another victim. He glanced up as she approached.

He looked as if he wanted to say something, but then shook his head and went back to work. She completely understood. There was nothing else they could do but continue providing care until more help arrived.

The wail of police sirens was a welcome relief. Yet after she quickly assessed those with more minor injuries, she forced herself to head back out to the street.

There were several people up on the flat bed of the truck, tending to the two ice skaters. She had to swallow hard against another wave of nausea when she saw blood dripping off the edge and onto the street. Somehow, she managed to climb up.

"We need to get her to the hospital," a man was saying. "They need to get Lifeline out here ASAP."

"Are you a doctor or nurse?" Elly asked. The way they'd mentioned the Lifeline rescue helicopter made her think so.

"I'm a doctor," the young woman said. "He's a nurse. The female skater is dead, but the male is still alive."

"Okay, you stay with him. I'll keep searching for other victims." Elly told herself the injured skater was in good hands. Much better hands than hers, that was for sure.

She wanted to cry when she found another dead body, an elderly man who'd taken a bullet to his chest. But after that, she was grateful to find two more live victims.

After stabilizing their injuries as much as she was able with her limited supplies, she helped them get over toward the ambulance. It seemed like the best place to keep them together.

As she worked, Elly couldn't stop thinking about Joe. Or

STRATEGIC THREAT 241

the man in the long dark coat who had done this terrible thing.

The man who she'd instinctively known was evil. Maybe even the devil himself.

---

JOE KINGSLEY HAD ONLY GOTTEN a glimpse of the shooter but tried to keep the brief image locked in his mind as he scoured the area searching for him. Using his radio, he'd alerted the other officers on duty, giving the brief description of short brown hair and long dark coat. Steele Delaney was the closest to him, and they'd fanned out, scanning the area for their shooter. Yet he couldn't deny the perp could have easily dumped the coat and even the weapon by now. And there were still far too many people milling about, running chaotically around the scene of the crime making it difficult to quarter the area for a grid search.

It wasn't easy to leave Elly behind. His boss and her older brother Rhy Finnegan would expect him to find and apprehend the shooter while also keeping Elly safe.

Ironic that she was the one to save him by shouting at him to get down a split second before the shooter fired another three rounds. Narrowly missing him and Elly.

They'd lost Kyle. After seeing the massive blood loss pooling beneath his fellow cop, he'd known the shooter must have hit an artery below the bullet-resistant vest they were all required to wear. The loss of a fellow tactical team member brought a fresh wave of anger. He'd been shocked and stunned when he'd heard the gunfire, then watched as the ice skaters went down on their small patch of ice.

These active shooter incidents were out of control. He'd never felt so helpless in his entire life.

All the more reason they needed to find this guy! Most shooters killed themselves or kept firing until a cop took them out. But not this guy. The fact that this shooter had sneaked away was outside the norm.

And he didn't like it. For all they knew, he'd escaped and was already planning his next shooting rampage. Maybe after he basked in the glow of his brutal success in taking out so many innocent victims. There was always an attention-seeking component to these events.

This one would be no different.

After a solid twenty minutes of searching, Joe, Steele, and Raelyn Lewis, the only three members of their team who had been assigned to the parade, had given up. He sent Steele and Raelyn out to scour for evidence, explaining his desire to check on Elly. Knowing Rhy would want that, too, the two cops had scattered to do what they could. He stood for a moment, considering what little he knew about their guy. The perp had seemed tall, but he had no way of knowing if the shooter had been standing up on a chair or some other object while firing into the crowd.

On his way back to Elly, he stopped and provided aid to several victims who were thankfully not hurt too badly. Then he noticed dozens of cops swarming the area and knew additional help had arrived.

Now that the immediate threat was over, at least as far as he could tell, Joe was impatient to get back to Elly. He desperately needed to know she was safe.

There was a growing crowd around the ambulance carrying the logo that matched Elly's uniform. He pushed forward, raking his gaze over the group of people until he found Elly's auburn hair.

A wave of relief hit hard, yet he didn't stop until he'd reached her side. "Elly? Are you okay?"

"Joe." She turned and grasped his arm, leaning against him for moment before letting him go. "Did you find him?"

"Not yet." He winced at the disappointment in her gaze. "You're sure you're not hurt?"

She gave a slight nod, but her gaze skittered from his. She looked so pale that he feared she had been hit and didn't realize it. He raked his eyes over her, finding plenty of blood smears, but nothing that appeared to be a recent injury.

"I saw him."

Her words were so soft with the chaos spewing around them, he wasn't sure he heard her correctly. He put his arm around her slim shoulders and pulled her close so he could speak into her ear. "What did you say?"

"I saw him." Her anguished gaze finally met his. "I literally bumped into him a few minutes before the parade started." She shook her head. "His blank, dead gaze made the hairs on the back of my neck stand up."

A cold chill that had nothing to do with the winter weather washed over him. "You saw him up close?"

She nodded. "I didn't know he had a gun or that he intended to hurt anyone. If I had, I would have told you or another cop. The minute I saw him, though, I felt he was evil. And now—this—" She broke off, biting her lip.

"He is evil." Joe was still struggling with the idea that she had seen the shooter. "Elly, we're going to need you to work with a sketch artist so we can get an ID on this guy. Can you do that for us?"

"Yes, of course." Her voice lacked conviction, but she nodded slowly. "I'll do whatever is necessary for you to find this guy before he hurts anyone else."

"I know you will." He cared for Elly, far more than he should considering she was his boss's youngest sister. She was off-limits in a big way. Not that it was easy to ignore her when they were together. He was about to pull away when his gaze landed on her name tag pinned to her uniform.

Finnegan.

He could almost hear Rhy screaming in his ear. This was not good. He pulled Elly closer. "We need to call your brother."

"What?" She stared at him as if he'd suggested they take a walk on the moon. "Don't be ridiculous. We need to search the area for more victims."

"Elly, this guy might figure out who you are." He couldn't quell a flash of panic. "You're wearing a name tag. People in Milwaukee have heard a lot about the Finnegan family over the past twelve months. You couldn't have gotten any more press coverage than if you were Hollywood superstars."

She gaped, speechless, then shook her head. "You're exaggerating. The shooter probably isn't from this area. I'm sure he chose the parade because it was a good target . . ." Her voice hitched, then trailed off at the grim realization of how this twisted mind had purposefully come to the Christmas parade because it would be the best place to kill a bunch of innocent people.

He didn't have a chance to say anything more because more officers and medically trained first responders converged on the scene. He tried to call Rhy, but the call went through to voice mail. He left a quick message saying Elly was fine but that they were at the scene of the Christmas parade where a gunman had opened fire.

Elly continued to provide care to those who came to the ambulance, while other medical providers stepped up to help triage. The scene was still chaotic, yet he didn't dare let Elly out of his sight. For one thing, he hadn't been kidding about needing her to work with a sketch artist to create a composite of this perp.

But even more so, he wasn't putting anything past this guy. The destruction surrounding them proved what he was capable of. She had bumped into the shooter, thought of him as evil because of the coldness in his eyes.

While wearing a name tag that announced she was a Finnegan.

The thing that bothered him the most was that the shooter didn't fit the profile of the average active shooter. They were mostly young white men, angry at the world, bigots who purposefully took out people of color. Taking their anger out on those who couldn't fight back.

The gunman he'd glimpsed from afar was older, maybe in his midthirties. And he hadn't stuck around to become famous, like so many other active shooters had.

He'd slipped away.

His phone buzzed a few minutes later. He edged away from the crowd, still keeping his gaze on Elly as he answered Rhy's call.

"You're sure she's not hurt?" Rhy demanded.

"I promise she's not injured." But Joe knew Elly was hurt deep inside. She was always smiling, full of fun and laughter, but today would likely have changed that for her.

And not for the better.

It made his heart ache, knowing she had lost her happy innocence.

"What happened?" Rhy was on vacation for the next two weeks over the holiday, or he would have been at the Christmas parade too. He shivered at the idea of Devon being here with their new baby.

He quickly filled Rhy in on the scant details he knew. Finally, he said, "The worst part is that Elly saw this guy up close. Apparently bumped into him. And, Rhy, she was wearing her uniform complete with her name tag."

There was a long tense silence on the other end of the line. Being on Rhy's team for the past five years, he knew very well that Finnegans didn't curse, but he could easily imagine Rhy wanting to. Maybe even saying the words in his head.

"Get her out of there, Kingsley. Bring her home."

"I will, but I'd like her to work with a sketch artist first." When Rhy didn't say anything, he added, "Rhy, the shooter is still out there. We need to find him."

"Yes, we do. But do me a favor, stick to Elly like glue."

"I will." He was glad Rhy was on board with the plan he'd already intended to carry out anyway. "I'm taking her to the police station now."

"Thanks, Joe." Rhy's tone was softer now. "I know I can trust you to take care of my baby sister."

"You can." He lifted his gaze up to the heavens above, vowing to make good on that promise.

No matter what.